TO DANCE WITH A PRINCE

BY
CARA COLTER

MILLS &
BOON

First published in Great Britain 2011
Harlequin Mills & Boon Limited,
Eton House, 18-24 Paradise Road, Richmond, Surrey TW9 1SR

© Cara Colter 2011

ISBN: 978 0 263 21978 4

Harlequin Mills & Boon policy is to use papers that are natural, renewable and recyclable products and made from wood grown in sustainable forests. The logging and manufacturing processes conform to the legal environmental regulations of the country of origin.

Printed and bound in Great Britain
by CPI Antony Rowe, Chippenham, Wiltshire

"Do you think there's anything in your world that could frighten me, Kiernan?

"I've been hungry. And so exhausted from working and raising a baby I couldn't even hold my feet under me. I've buried my child. And my mother. Do you think anything in your cozy, pampered little world could scare me? The press? I could handle the press with both my hands tied behind my back.

"Don't pretend you're just trying to protect me. Your Royal Highness, you are protecting yourself. You don't want anyone to know about me. I'm a sullied girl from the wrong side of the tracks. What an embarrassment to you! To be romantically linked to the likes of me!"

"I have told you everything there is to know about me," Kiernan said quietly, "and you would reach that conclusion?"

"That's right!" she snapped, her anger making her feel so much more powerful than her despair. "It's all about you!"

Meredith banished everything in her that was weak. There would be plenty of time for crying when she got home. Because she realized she had done the dumbest thing of her whole life. She had come to love a real prince. And she did not think she could survive another love going wrong.

Dear Reader

It is such an incredible time of year here in British Columbia. The scent of lilacs fills the air, the flower buds are full and round, and the horses are kicking up their heels in lush green pasture. Spring is such a gorgeous time of renewal and hope, and yet... weeding needs to be done. The lawnmower breaks. A family member is sick. An unexpected bill comes in. A grandchild is going through a heart-wrenching challenge.

That is what I love about a good book. It provides that moment to pause, to plump up the pillows on the bed, crawl in, and be whisked away to a wonderful fantasy world.

So I hope you'll regard the book in your hands as an invitation. Slip away. Come play. Take a mini-vacation with me to the Isle of Chatam, meet the man who will be King, and the ordinary woman who can see through his armour to his heart.

And I promise when you come back from this storybook holiday you'll have felt the triumph of love, and you'll be so much more ready to tackle whatever challenges your life holds today. I'm honoured, as always, to be part of your journey.

With love

Cara

Cara Colter lives on an acreage in British Columbia with her partner, Rob, and eleven horses. She has three grown children and a grandson. She is a recent recipient of the *RT Book Reviews* Career Achievement Award in the 'Love and Laughter' category. Cara loves to hear from readers, and you can contact her or learn more about her through her website: www.cara-colter.com

To Rose and Bill Pastorek
with heartfelt thanks for creating
such an incredible garden, a 'mini-vacation'
for everyone who experiences it.

CHAPTER ONE

THE HOWL OF PURE PAIN sent icicles down Prince Kiernan of Chatam's spine. He shot through the door of the palace infirmary, and came to a halt when he saw his cousin, Prince Adrian, lying on a cot, holding his knee and squirming in obvious agony.

"I told you that horse was too much for you!" Kiernan growled.

"Nice to see you, too," Adrian gasped. "Naturally, the moment you told me the horse was too much for me, my fate was sealed."

Kiernan shook his head, knowing it was all too true. His cousin, seven years his junior, was twenty-one, reckless, but usually easily able to deflect the consequences of his recklessness with his abundance of charm.

A fact Adrian proved by smiling bravely at a young nurse. Satisfied that the girl was close to swooning, he turned his attention back to Kiernan.

"Look, if you could spare me the lecture," Adrian said, "I am in desperate need of a favor. I'm supposed to be somewhere."

First of all, his cousin was never desperate. Secondly, Adrian rarely worried about where he was supposed to be.

"DH—that's short for Dragon-heart—is going to kill

me if I'm not there. Honestly, Kiernan, I've met the most fearsome woman who ever walked."

And thirdly, as far as Kiernan knew his cousin had never met a woman, fearsome or not, he could not slay with his devil-may-care grin.

"Do you think you could stand in for me?" Adrian pleaded. "Just this once?" The nurse probed his alarmingly swollen knee, and Adrian howled again.

What Kiernan was having trouble fathoming was how Adrian, who would be the first to admit he was entirely self-focused, was managing to think about *anything* at this particular moment besides his injury.

"Just cancel," Kiernan suggested.

"She'll think I did it on purpose," Adrian said through clenched teeth.

"Nobody would think you had an accident on purpose to inconvenience them."

"*She* would. DH, aka Meredith Whitmore. She snorts fire." An almost dreamy look pierced Adrian's pain. "Though her breath is actually more like mint."

Kiernan was beginning to wonder what his cousin had been given for pain.

"The fact is," Adrian said sadly, " DH eats adorable little princes like me for her lunch. Barbecued. She must have the mint after."

"What on earth are you talking about?"

"You remember Sergeant Major Henderson?"

"Hard to forget," Kiernan said dryly of the man in charge of taking youthful princes and turning them into disciplined, rock-hard warriors, capable of taking commands as well as giving them.

"Meredith Whitmore is him. The Sergeant Major. Times ten," Adrian said, and then whimpered when his knee was probed again.

"You're exaggerating. You must be."

"Would you just stand in for me? Please?"

"What would make me agree to stand in for you with a woman who likes her princes barbecued and who makes Sergeant Major Henderson look like a Girl Scout leader? I don't even know what I'm standing in *for.*"

"It was a mistake," Adrian admitted sadly. "I thought it was going to be a lark. It sounded like so much more fun than some of the other official *lesser prince* options for Chatam Blossom Week."

Blossom Week was the Isle of Chatam's annual celebration of spring. Dating back to medieval times, it was a week-long festival that started with a fund-raising gala and ended with a royal ball. Opening night was a little over a week away.

Adrian continued, "I could have given out awards to the preschool percussion band, given the Blossom Week rah-rah speech *or* done a little dance. Which would you have picked?"

"Probably the speech," Kiernan said. "Have you given him something?"

"Not yet," the nurse said pleasantly, "but I'm about to."

"Lucky you," Adrian said, batting his eyes at her, "because I have the cutest little royal backside—ouch! Was that unnecessarily rough?"

"Don't be a baby, Your Highness."

Adrian watched her walk away. "Anyway, I said I'd learn a dance. I was going to perform with an up-and-coming troupe at the fund-raising evening. It's a talent show this year. My suggestion to call the fund-raiser *Raise a Little Hell* was vetoed. Naturally. It's going to be called *An Evening to Remember*, which I think is *totally* forgettable."

"I'm not taking your place for a dance number! We both know I can't dance. Prince of Heartaches causes Foot Aches, Too." It was a direct quote from a newspaper headline, with a very unflattering picture of Kiernan crushing some poor girl's foot at her debutante ball.

"Ah, the press is hard on you, Kiernan. They never nickname me. But in the past ten years you've been the Playboy Prince—"

That had been when Kiernan was eighteen, fresh out of an all-boys private school, one summer of freedom before his military training. He had been, unfortunately, like a kid let out in a candy shop!

"Then, the Prince of Heartaches."

At the age of twenty-three, Prince Kiernan had become engaged to one of his oldest and dearest friends, Francine Lacourte. Not even Adrian knew the full truth behind their split and her total disappearance from public life. But, given a history that the press was eager not to let him shake, it was assumed Prince Kiernan was to blame.

"Now," Adrian continued, "since Tiff, you've graduated to Prince Heartbreaker. Tut-tut. It would all lead one to believe you are so much more exciting than you are."

Kiernan scowled warningly at his cousin.

"Don't give me that look," Adrian said, whatever the nurse had given him relaxing the grimace on his face to a decidedly goofy grin. "Your tiff with Tiff."

While the press *loved* the high-spirited high jinks of Adrian, Kiernan was seen as too stern, and too serious. Particularly since two broken engagements to two very popular women he was seen as coldly remote.

He knew the title Prince Heartbreaker was probably going to be his mantle to bear forever, even if he lived out the rest of his days as a monk, which, after what he'd been through, didn't seem entirely unappealing!

After all, the future of his island nation rested solidly and solely on Kiernan's shoulders, as he was the immediate successor to his mother, Queen Aleda's, throne. That kind of responsibility was enough for one man to bear without throwing in the caprice of romance.

Adrian was fourth in line, a position he found deliciously relaxing.

"You should have thrown that Tiffany Wells under a bus," Adrian said with a sigh. "She deserved it. Imagine tricking you into thinking she was pregnant. And then do you let the world know the true reason for the broken engagement? Oh, no, a man of honor—"

"We're not talking about this," Kiernan said fiercely. Then, hoping to get back on one topic and off the other, "Look, Adrian, about the dancing thing, I don't see how I could help—"

"I don't ask much of you, Kiern."

That was true. The whole world came to Kiernan, asking, begging, requesting, pleading causes. Adrian never did.

"Do this, okay?" Adrian said, his words beginning to slur around the edges. "It'll be good for you. Even if you make a fool of yourself, it'll make you seem human."

"I don't seem human?" He pretended to be affronted.

His cousin ignored him. "A little soft shoe, charm the crowd, get a little good press for a change. It bugs the hell out of me that you're constantly portrayed as a coldhearted snob."

"Coldhearted? A snob?" He pretended to be wounded.

Again, he was ignored. "That's if you can survive the fire-breather. Who, by the way, doesn't like tardiness.

And you…" his unfocused eyes shifted to the clock, and he squinted thoughtfully at it "…are twenty-two minutes late. She's waiting in the Ballroom."

The smart thing to do, Kiernan knew, as he left his cousin, would be to send someone to tell the fire-breather Adrian was hurt.

But the truth was he had yet to see a woman who had managed to intimidate Adrian. Because if Kiernan was legendary for his remoteness, his cousin was just as legendary for his charm.

The press loved Prince Adrian. He played Prince Charming to his darker cousin's Prince Heartbreaker. And, oh, how women loved Prince Adrian.

Kiernan just had to see the one who did not.

Kiernan decided to go have a look at Adrian's nemesis before giving Adrian's excuses and dismissing her. In his most warmhearted and non-snobby fashion.

Meredith glared at the clock.

"He's late," she muttered to herself. The truth? She couldn't believe it! It was the second time Prince Adrian had been tardy!

She'd been intimidated by the young prince and his status for all of about ten seconds at their first meeting at her upscale downtown Chatam dance and fitness studio.

And then she'd seen he was like a puppy—using the fact he was totally adorable to have his way! Including being late. Meredith was so beyond being charmed by a man, even one as cute as him.

So, she'd laid down the law with him. And she'd been certain he wouldn't dare be late again, especially since she had conceded to changing their meeting place to the Chatam Palace Great Ballroom as a convenience to him.

Which just showed how wrong she could be when it came to men, even while she thought she was totally immune to sexy good looks and impossible charm!

Meredith glanced around the grandeur of the room and tried not to be overly awed at finding herself here.

She breathed in the familiar scents of her childhood. Her mother, a single woman, had been a cleaning lady. Meredith recognized the aromas of freshly shined floors, furniture wax, glass cleaners, silver polish.

Her mother would have been as awed by this room as Meredith was. Her mother had dreamed such big dreams for her daughter.

Ballet will open doors to worlds we can hardly imagine, Merry.

Worlds just like this one, Meredith thought gazing around the room. Wouldn't her mother be thrilled to know she was here?

Because every door that ballet could have opened for Meredith—and her mother—had slammed shut when Meredith had found herself pregnant at sixteen.

Morning sunshine streamed in the twelve floor-to-ceiling arched windows that were so clean they looked like they contained no glass. The light glinted across the Italian marble of the floors, and sparked in the thousands of Swarovski crystals of the three huge chandeliers that dangled from the frescoed ceiling.

Meredith glanced again at the clock.

Prince Adrian was half an hour late. He wasn't coming. Meredith had had her doubts about this whole scheme, but been persuaded by the wild enthusiasm of the girls.

Crazy to let the teenage girls, the ones she mentored

and loved and taught to dance, younger versions of herself, believe in fairy-tale dreams.

She, of all people, should know better.

Still, looking around this room, something stirred in her. She was going to dance here, prince or no prince.

In fact, that would be very in keeping with the charity she had founded, that gave her reason to go on, when all of her life had crashed down around her.

Meredith taught upbeat modern dancing as part of the program No Princes, which targeted the needs of underprivileged inner city female adolescents.

"You don't need a prince to dance," Meredith said firmly. In fact, that would make a good motto for the group. Perhaps she should consider adding it to their letterhead.

She closed her eyes. In her imagination, she could hear music begin to play. She had broken with ballet years ago, not just because her scholarship had been canceled. When she finally returned to dance, the only place that could ease the hurt of a heart snapped in two, she had found she could not handle the rigidity of ballet. She needed a place where her emotion could come out.

But even so, Meredith found herself doing the famous entrée of Princess Aurora in the Petipa/Tchaikovsky ballet, *The Sleeping Beauty*.

But then, she let the music take her, and she seamlessly joined the *allegro* movements of ballet with the modern dance that had become her specialty. She melded different styles of dance together, creating something brand new, feeling herself being taken to the only place where she was not haunted by memories.

Meredith covered the floor on increasingly light feet,

twirling, twisting, leaping, part controlled, part wild, wholly uninhibited.

She became aware that dancing in this great room felt like a final gift to the mother she had managed to disappoint so terribly.

The music that played in her head stopped and she became still, but for a moment she did not open her eyes, just savored the feeling of having been with her mother for a moment, embraced by her, all that had gone sour between them made right.

And then Meredith could have sworn she heard a baby laugh.

She spun around just as the complete silence of the room was broken by a single pair of hands clapping.

"How dare you?" she said, feeling as if Prince Adrian had spied on her in a very private moment.

And then Meredith realized it was the wrong prince!

It was not Adrian, eager and clumsily enthusiastic, like a playful St. Bernard, but the man who would be king.

Prince Heartbreaker.

Prince Kiernan of Chatam had slipped inside the door, and stood with his back braced lazily against the richness of the walnut. The crinkle of amusement around the deep azure of his eyes disappeared at her reprimand.

"How dare I? Excuse me. I thought I was in my own home." He looked astonished, rather than annoyed, by her reprimand.

"I'm sorry, Your Highness," she stammered. "I was taken off guard. That dance was never intended for anyone to see."

"More's the pity," he said mildly.

Meredith saw, instantly, that the many pictures of him printed by papers and tabloids did not begin to do him justice. And she saw why he was called Prince Heartbreaker.

Such astonishing good looks should be illegal. Paired with his station in life, it seemed quite possible he could break hearts with a glance!

Prince Kiernan was more than gorgeous, he was stunning. Tall and exquisitely fit, his perfectly groomed hair was crisp and dark, his face chiseled masculine perfection, from the cut of high cheekbones to the jut of a perfectly clefted chin.

Though he was dressed casually—it looked like he had been riding, the tan-colored jodhpurs hugging the cut of the muscle of his thigh—nothing could hide the supreme confidence of his bearing.

He was a man who had been born to great wealth and privilege and it showed in every single thing about him. But an underlying strength—around the stern line of his mouth, the way he held his broad shoulders—also showed.

And Meredith Whitmore was, suddenly, not an accomplished dancer and a successful businesswoman, but the cleaning lady's daughter, who had been trained to be invisible in front of her "betters," who had stupidly thrown her life away on a dream that had ended more badly than she ever could have imagined.

She thought of the unleashed sensuousness of that dance, and felt a fire burn up her cheeks. She prayed—desperately—for the floor to open up and swallow her.

But she, of all people, should know by now that the desperation of a prayer in no way led to its answer.

"Your Royal Highness," she said, and all her grace fled her as she did a clumsy curtsy.

"You can't be Meredith Whitmore," the prince said, clearly astounded.

"I can't?"

Even his voice—cultured, deep, melodic, masculine—was unfairly attractive, as sensual as a touch.

It was no wonder she was questioning her own identity!

Meredith *begged* the confident, career-oriented woman she had become to push the embarrassed servant's daughter off center stage. She begged the vulnerability that the memory of Carly's laugh had brought to the surface to go away.

"Why can't I be Meredith Whitmore?" Despite her effort to speak with careless confidence, she thought she sounded like a rejected actress who had been refused a coveted role.

"From what Adrian said, I was expecting, um, a female version of Attila the Hun."

"Flattering."

A hint of a smile raced across the firm line of those stern lips and then was gone.

It was definitely a smile that could break hearts. Meredith reminded herself, firmly, she hadn't one to break!

"You did give me a hard time for standing inside my own door," he said thoughtfully. "Adrian said, er, that you were something of a taskmaster."

The hesitation said it all. Meredith guessed that Prince Adrian had not worded it that politely. The fact that the two princes had discussed her—in unflattering terms—made her wish for the floor to open up redouble.

"I was actually about to leave," she said with the

haughtiness of a woman who was not the least vulnerable to him, and whose time was extremely valuable—which it was! "He's very late."

"I'm afraid he's not coming. He sent me with the message."

Meredith felt a shiver of apprehension. "Is it just for today? That Prince Adrian isn't coming?"

But somehow she already knew the answer. And it was her fault. She had driven him too hard. She had overstepped herself. He didn't want to do it anymore. She had obviously been too bossy, too intense, too driven to perfection.

A female version of Attila the Hun.

"I'm sorry. He's been injured in an accident."

"Badly?" Meredith asked. The prince, puppylike in his eagerness to please, had been hurt, and all she was thinking about was that she was being inconvenienced by his tardiness?

"He's been in a riding accident. When I left him his knee was the approximate size and shape of a basketball."

Meredith marshaled herself, not wanting him to see her flinch from the blow to her plans, to her girls.

"Well, as terrible as that is," she said with all the composure she could muster, "the show must go on. I'm sure with a little resourcefulness we can rewrite the part. We aren't called No Princes for nothing."

"No Princes? Is that the name of your dance troupe, then?"

"It is actually more than a dance troupe."

"All right," he conceded. "I'm intrigued. Tell me more."

To her surprise, the prince looked authentically interested. Despite not wanting to be vulnerable to him in any way, Meredith took a deep breath, knowing she could not pass up this opportunity to tell someone so influential about her group.

"No Princes is an organization that targets girls from the tough neighborhoods of the inner city of Chatam. At fifteen and sixteen and seventeen a frightening number of these girls, still children really, are much too eager to leave school, and have babies, instead of getting their education."

Her story, *exactly*, but there was no reason to tell him that part.

"We try to give them a desire to learn, marketable skills, and a strong sense of self-reliance and self-sufficiency. We hope to influence them so they do not feel they need rescuing from their circumstances by the first boy they perceive as a prince!"

Michael Morgan had been that prince for her. He had been new to the neighborhood, drifted in from somewhere with a sexy Australian accent. She was fatherless, craving male attention, susceptible.

And thanks to him, she would never be that vulnerable again. Though the man who stood before her would certainly be a test of any woman's resolve to not believe in fairy tales.

"And where do you fit into that vision, my gypsy ballerina?"

So, the prince *had* seen something. *His* gypsy ballerina? Some terrible awareness of him tingled along her spine, but she kept her tone entirely professional when she answered him. She, of all people, knew that tingle to be a warning sign.

"I'm afraid all work and no play is a poor equation for anyone, never mind these girls. As well as looking after a lot of paperwork for No Princes, I get to do the *fun* part. I teach the girls how to dance."

"Prince Adrian didn't seem to think it was fun," he said dryly.

"I may have pushed him a little hard," she admitted.

Prince Kiernan actually laughed, and it changed everything. Did the papers deliberately capture him looking grim and humorless?

Because in that spontaneous shout of laughter Meredith had an unfortunate glimpse of the kind of man every woman hoped would ride in on his white charger to rescue her from her life.

Even a woman such as herself, soured on romance, could feel the pull of his smile. She steeled herself against that traitorous flutter in her breast and reminded herself a man did not get the name Prince Heartbreaker because he was in the market for a princess!

In fact, before he'd been called Prince Heartbreaker, hadn't he been called the Playboy Prince? And something else? Oh, yes, the Prince of Heartaches. He was a dangerous, dangerous man.

"Kudos to you if you *could* push him hard," Prince Kiernan said wryly. "How did Adrian come to be a part of all this?"

It was a relief to hide behind words! They provided the veneer of rational, civilized thought, when something rebellious in her was reacting to him in a very upsettingly primal way!

"One of our girls, Erin Fisher, wrote a dance number that really tells the whole story of what No Princes does. It's quite a remarkable piece. It takes girls from hanging out on street corners flirting with boys, going nowhere, to a place of remarkable strength and admirable ambition. The piece has a dream sequence in it that shows a girl dancing with a prince.

"Unbeknownst to any of us, Erin sent it to the palace, along with a video of the girls dancing, as a performance suggestion for *An Evening to Remember*, the fund-raiser that will open Blossom Week. She very boldly suggested Prince Adrian for the part in the dream sequence. The girls have been delirious since he accepted."

Meredith was shocked by the sudden emotion that clawed at her throat. She shouldn't have a favorite, but of all the girls, Erin was so much like her, so bright, so full of potential. And so sensitive. So easily hurt and discouraged.

"I'm sorry for their disappointment," Prince Kiernan said, making Meredith realize, uneasily, he was reading her own disappointment with way too much accuracy.

Prince Kiernan was larger than life. He was *better* than the pictures. His voice was as sexy as a piece of raw silk scraped along the nape of a neck. He was a *real* prince.

But still, she represented No Princes. She *taught* young women not to get swept away, not to believe in fairy tales. She rescued the vulnerable from throwing their lives away on fantasies, as she had, no matter how appealing the illusion.

The abundance of tabloid pictures of actress Tiffany Wells' tearstained face since her broken engagement with this man underscored Meredith's determination not to be vulnerable in any way, to any man, ever again.

Her days of vulnerability were over.

"A little disappointment does nothing but build character," she said crisply.

He regarded her thoughtfully. She thrust her chin up and folded her arms over her chest.

"Again, I'm sorry."

"It's quite all right," she said, forcing her voice to be firm. "Things happen that are out of our control."

She would have snatched those words back without speaking them if she knew that they would swing the door of memory wide open on the event in her life that had been most out of her control.

Meredith slammed the door shut again, blinking hard and swallowing.

The prince was looking at her way too closely, again, as if he could see things she would not have him see. That she would not have anyone see.

"Goodbye," Meredith managed to squeak out. "Thank you for coming personally, Your Highness. I'll let the girls know. We'll figure something out. It's not a big deal."

She was babbling, trying to outrun the quiver in her voice and failing. She kept talking.

"The girls will get over it. In fact, they're used to it. They're used to disappointment. As I said, we can re-write the part Prince Adrian was going to play. Anybody can play a prince."

Though she might have believed that much more strongly before standing in the damnably charismatic presence of a real one!

"Goodbye," she said, more strongly, a hint for him to go. The quiver was out of her voice, but she had not slammed the door on her worst memory as completely as she had hoped. She could feel tears sparking behind her eyes.

But Prince Kiernan wasn't moving. It was probably somewhere in that stuffy royal protocol book she'd been given that she wasn't supposed to turn her back on him first, that she wasn't to dismiss *him*, but she had to. She had to escape him gazing at her so piercingly, as if her whole life story was playing in her eyes and he could see it. It would only be worse if she cried.

She turned swiftly and began pack up the music equipment she had brought in preparation for her session with Adrian.

She waited for the sound of footfalls, the whisper of the door opening and shutting.

But it didn't come.

CHAPTER TWO

MEREDITH DREW TWO OR THREE steadying breaths. Only when she was sure no tears would fall did she turn back. Prince Kiernan still stood there.

She almost yearned for a lecture about protocol, but there was no recrimination in his eyes.

"It meant a lot to them, didn't it?" he asked quietly, his voice rich with sympathy, "And especially to you."

She had to steel herself against how accurately he had read her emotion, but at least he didn't have a clue as to why she was really feeling so deeply.

It felt like her survival depended on not letting on that it was a personal pain that had touched her off emotionally. So, again, she tried to hide behind words. Meredith launched into a speech she had given a thousand times to raise funds for No Princes.

"You have to understand how marginalized these girls feel. Invisible. Lacking in value. Most of them are from single-parent families, and that parent is a mother. It's part of what makes them so vulnerable when the first boy winks at them and tells them they're beautiful.

"So when a prince, when a real live prince, one of the biggest celebrities on our island recognized what they were doing as having worth, it was incredible. I think it made them have hope that their dreams really could come true. That's a hard sell in Wentworth. Hope is a dangerous thing in that world."

Kiernan's face registered Wentworth. He *knew* the name of the worst neighborhood on his island. She had successfully diverted him from her own moment of intense vulnerability.

But before she could finish congratulating herself, Prince Kiernan took a deep breath, ran a hand through the crisp silk of his dark hair.

"Hope shouldn't be a dangerous thing," he said softly, finally looking back at her. "Not in anyone's world."

Honestly, the man could make you melt if you weren't on guard. Thankfully, Meredith's life had made her stronger than that! She had seen lives—including her own—ruined by weakness, by that single moment of giving in to temptation.

And this man was a temptation!

Well, not really. Not realistically. He was a prince, and she was a servant's daughter. Some things did not mix, even in this liberated age. Her roots were in the poorest part of his kingdom. She was not an unsullied virgin. She had known tragedy beyond her years. It had taken away her ability to dream, to believe.

The only thing she believed in was her girls at No Princes. The only thing that gave her reprieve from her pain was dancing.

No, there were no fairy tales for her.

She did not rely on anyone but herself, and certainly not a man, not even a prince. That was why she had been so immune to Prince Adrian's charms.

Merry, Merry, Merry, she could almost hear her mother's weary, bitter voice, *when in all your life has a man ever done the right thing?*

Her mother had been so right.

So Prince Kiernan shocked Meredith now. By being the one man willing to do the right thing.

"I'll do it," he said with a certain grim resolve, like a man volunteering to face the firing squad. "I'll take Prince Adrian's place."

Meredith felt her mouth open, and then snapped shut again. There was no joy in the prince's offer, only a sense of obligation.

Naturally I'll marry you, Michael had lied to her when Meredith had told him about the coming baby.

Oh, darlin', pigs will fly before that man's going to marry you. You're dreaming, girl.

Meredith had a feeling the prince would *never* run out on his obligations. Still, she had to discourage him.

Teaching Prince Adrian the steps to the dream sequence dance had been one thing. Despite his royal status, working with the young prince had been something like dealing with a slightly unruly younger brother.

This man was not like that.

There were things a whole lot more dangerous than hope.

And Prince Kiernan of Chatam, the Playboy Prince, the Prince of Heartaches, Prince Heartbreaker, was one of them.

"It's not a good idea," Meredith said. "Thank you, anyway, but no."

The prince looked shocked that anyone could turn down such a generous offer. And then downright annoyed.

"You just have no idea how much work is involved," Meredith said, a last ditch effort to somehow save herself. "Prince Adrian had committed to several hours a day. We have just over a week left until *An Evening to Remember.* I don't see how we could get you caught up. Really." He didn't seem to be hearing her, so she repeated, "Thanks, but no."

Prince Kiernan crossed the room to her. Closer, she could see his great height. The man towered over her. His scent was drugging.

But not as much as the light in those amazing blue eyes. Still cool, there was something powerful there. His gaze locked on her face and held her fast in a spell.

"Do I look like a man who is afraid of work?" he asked, softly, challengingly.

The truth? He didn't have a clue what work was. He wouldn't know it probably took a team of people hours on their hands and knees to polish these floors, to clean the windows, to make the crystals on the chandeliers sparkle like diamonds.

But she didn't say that because when she looked into his face she saw raw strength beneath the sophisticated surface. She saw resolve.

And Meredith saw exactly what he was offering. He was *saving* the dreams of all the girls. As much as she did not want to be exposed to all this raw masculine energy every single day for the next week, was this really her choice to make?

Ever since Prince Adrian had agreed to dance in *her* production, Erin had dreamed bigger. Her marks at school had become astonishing. She had mentioned, shyly, to Meredith, she might think of becoming a doctor.

Meredith couldn't throw away the astonishing gift Prince Kiernan was offering her girls because she felt threatened, vulnerable.

Still, her eyes fastened on the sensuous curve of his full lower lip.

God? Don't do this to me.

But she already knew she was not on the list of those who had their prayers answered.

The prince surprised her by smiling, though it only intensified her thought, of *don't do this to me.*

"I'm afraid," he said, "it's probably you who doesn't know how much work will be involved. I have been called the Prince of Foot Aches. And you have only a short time to turn that around? Poor girl."

His smile heightened her sense of danger, of something spinning out of her control. Meredith wanted, with a kind of desperation, to tell him this could not possibly work.

Dance with him every day? Touch him, and look at him, and somehow not be sucked into all the romantic longings a close association to such a dynamic and handsome man was bound to stir up?

But she had all her pain to keep her strong, a fortress of grief whose walls she could hide behind.

And she thought of Erin Fisher, and the girl she herself used to be. Meredith thought about hopes and dreams, and the excited delirium of the dance troupe.

"Thank you, Your Highness," she said formally. "When would you be able to begin?"

Prince Kiernan had jumped out of airplanes, participated in live-round military exercises, flown a helicopter.

He had ridden highly strung ponies on polo fields and jumped horses over the big timbers of steeplechases.

He had sailed solo in rough water, ocean kayaked and done deep-sea dives. The truth was he did not lead a life devoid of excitement and, in fact, had confronted fear often.

What came as a rather unpleasant surprise to him

was the amount of trepidation he felt about *dancing*, of all things.

He knew at least part of that trepidation was due to the fact he had made the offer to help the No Princes dance troupe on an impulse. His plan, he recalled, had been to see the Dragon-heart with his own eyes, make Prince Adrian's excuses, and then dismiss the dance instructor.

One thing Prince Kiernan of Chatam was not, was impulsive. He did not often veer from the plan. It was the one luxury he could not afford.

That eighteenth summer, his year of restless energy, heady lack of restraint, and impulsive self-indulgence had taught him that for him, spontaneity was always going to have a price.

The military had given him an outlet for all that pent-up energy and replaced impulsiveness with discipline.

Those years after his eighteenth birthday had reinforced his knowledge that his life did not really belong to him. Every decision was weighed and measured cautiously in terms, not of his well-being, but the well-being of his small island nation. There was little room for spontaneity in a world that was highly structured and carefully planned. His schedule of appointments and royal obligations sometimes stretched years in advance.

Aware he was *always* watched and judged, Kiernan had become a man who was calm and cool, absolutely controlled in every situation. His life was public, his demeanor was always circumspect. Unlike his cousin, he did not have the luxury of emotional outbursts when things did not go his way. Unlike his cousin, he could not pull pranks, be late, forget appointments.

He was rigidly *correct*, and if his training and inborn sense of propriety did not exactly inspire warm fuzziness, it did inspire confidence. People knew they could trust him and trust his leadership. Even after Francine, the whispers of what had happened to her, people seemed to give him the benefit of the doubt and trust him, still.

But then his relationship with Tiffany Wells, an exception to the amount of control he exerted over his life, seemed to have damaged that trust. His reputation had escalated from that of a man who was coolly remote to a man who was a heartless love-rat.

There would be no more losses of control.

And while it was not high on his list of priorities to be popular, he did see performing the dance as an opportunity to repair a battered image. His and Tiffany's breakup was a year ago. It was time for people to see him as capable of having a bit of fun, relaxing, being human.

Was that why he'd said yes? A public relations move? An opportunity to polish a tarnished image, as Adrian had suggested?

No.

Was it because of the girls, then? He had been moved by Miss Whitmore's description of the goals of No Princes. Kiernan had felt a very real surge of compassion for underprivileged young women who wanted someone they perceived as important to value them, to recognize what they were doing as having merit.

But had that been the reason he had said yes? The reason he had been swayed to this unlikely cause that was certainly going to require more of him than signing a cheque, or giving a speech or just showing up and shaking a few hands? Was that the reason he'd said yes to a cause that had his staff running in circles trying to rearrange his appointments around his new schedule? Again, *no*.

So, was it her, then? Was Meredith Whitmore the reason he had said *yes* to something so far out of his comfort zone?

Kiernan let his mind go to her. She had astounding hazel eyes, that hinted at fire, unconsciously pouty lips, a smattering of light freckles and a wild tangle of auburn locks, the exact kind of hair that made a man's hands itch to touch.

Add to that the lithe dancer's body dressed in a leotard that clung to long, lean legs, and a too-large T-shirt that hinted at, rather than revealed, luscious curves. There was simply no denying she was attractive, but not in the way one might expect of a dancer. She was at odds with the dance he had witnessed, because she seemed more uptight than Bohemian, more Sergeant Major than free-spirited gypsy.

Beautiful? Undoubtedly. But the truth was he was wary of beauty, rather than enchanted by it, particularly after Tiffany. The face of an angel had hidden a twisted heart, capable of deception that had rattled his world.

Meredith Whitmore did not look capable of deception, but there was something about her he didn't get. She was young, and yet her eyes were shadowed, cool, measuring.

Not exactly cold, but Kiernan could understand why Adrian had called her Dragon-heart, like something fierce burned at her core that you would get close to at your own peril.

So, he had said yes, not because it would be a good public relations move, which it would be, not wholly on the grounds of compassion, though it was that, and not because of Meredith's beauty or mystery. It was not even her very obvious emotional reaction to her disappointment and her valiant effort to hide that from him.

No, he thought frowning, the answer to his agreeing to this was somewhere in those first moments when she had been dancing, unaware of his presence. But what *exactly* it was that had been so compelling as to overcome his characteristic aversion to spontaneity eluded him.

So, the astounding fact was that Prince Kiernan, the most precise of men, could not pinpoint precisely what had made him agree to do this. And the fact that he could not decipher his own motivations was deeply disturbing to him.

Now, he paused at the doorway of the ballroom, took a deep breath, put back his shoulders, and strode in.

He hoped to find her dancing, knowing the answer was in that, but she was not to be caught off guard twice.

Meredith was fiddling with electronic equipment in one corner of the huge ballroom, her tongue caught between her teeth, her brow drawn down in a scowl. She looked up and saw him, straightened.

"Miss Whitmore," he said.

She was wearing purple tights today, rumpled leg warmers, and a hairband of an equally hideous shade of purple held auburn curls off her face. She didn't have on a speck of makeup. She did have on an oversized lime green T-shirt that said, *Don't kiss any frogs.*

He was used to people trying to impress him, at least a little bit, but she was obviously dressed only for comfort and for the work ahead. He wasn't quite sure if he was charmed or annoyed by her lack of effort to look appealing.

And he wasn't quite sure if he felt charmed or annoyed that she looked appealing anyway!

"Prince Kiernan," she said, a certain coolness in her tone, which was mirrored in the amazing green gold of those eyes, "thank you for rearranging your schedule for this."

"I did as much as I could. I may have to take the occasional official phone call."

"Understandable. Thank you for being on time."

"I'm always on time." He could see why she intimidated Adrian. No greeting, no polite *how are you today?* There was a no-nonsense tone to her voice that reminded him of a palace tutor. He could certainly hear a hint of Dragon-heart in there!

"Brilliant," she said, and then stood back, folded her arms over her chest, and inspected him. Now he could also see a hint of Sergeant Henderson as her brows lowered in disapproval! He felt like he had showed up for a military exercise in full dress uniform when the dress of the day was combat attire.

"Do those slacks have some give to them? I brought some dance pants, just in case."

Dance pants? He disliked that uncharacteristic moment of spontaneity that had made him say yes to this whole idea more by the second. He wasn't going to ask her what dance pants were, exactly. He was fairly certain he could guess.

"I'm sure these will be fine," he said stiffly, in a voice that let her know a prince did not discuss his *pants* with a maiden, no matter how fair.

She looked doubtful, but shrugged and turned to the electronics. "I have this video I want you to watch, if you don't mind, Your Highness."

As he came and stood beside her, the scent of lemons

tickled his nostrils. She flicked a switch on a bright pink laptop. The light from the chandeliers danced in her hair, making the red threads in it spark like fire.

"This has had twelve million hits," she said, accessing a video-sharing website.

He focused on a somewhat grainy video of a wedding celebration. A large room had a crowd standing around the edges of it, a space cleared in the center of it for a youthful-looking bride and groom.

"And now for the first dance," a voice announced.

The groom took one of his bride's hands, placed his other with a certain likeable awkwardness on her silk-clad waist.

"This is the bridal waltz," Meredith told him, "and it's a very traditional three-step waltz."

The young groom began to shuffle around the dance floor.

Kiernan felt relieved. The groom danced just like him. "Nothing to learn," he pronounced, "I can already do that." He looked at his watch. "Maybe I can squeeze in a ride before lunch."

"I've already lost one prince to riding," she said without looking up from the screen. "No riding until we're done the performance."

Kiernan felt a shiver of pure astonishment, and looked at Meredith Whitmore again, harder. She didn't appear to notice.

She tacked on a *"Your Highness"* as if that made bossing him around perfectly acceptable. Well, it wasn't as if Adrian hadn't warned him.

"Excuse me, but I really didn't sign up to have you run my—"

Meredith shushed him as if he was a schoolboy. "This part's important."

He was so startled that he thought he might laugh out loud. No one, but no one, talked to him like that. He slid her a look as if he was seeing her for the first time. She *was* bossy. And what's worse, she was *cute* when she was bossy.

Not that he would let her know that. He reached by her, and clicked on the pause button on the screen.

It was her turn to be startled, but he had her full attention. And he was not falling under the spell of those haunting gold-green eyes.

"I am already giving you two hours a day of practice time that I can barely afford," he told her sternly. "You will not tell me what to do with the rest of my time. Are we clear?"

Rather than looking clear, she looked mutinous.

"I've set aside a certain amount of my time for you, not given you run of my life." There. That should remind her a little gratitude would not be out of order.

But she did not look grateful, or cowed, either. In fact, Meredith Whitmore looked downright peeved.

"I've set aside a certain amount of time for you, also," she announced haughtily. "I'm not investing more of my time to have you end up out of commission, too! We're on a very limited schedule because of Prince Adrian's horse mishap."

Prince Kiernan looked at Meredith closely. Right behind the annoyance in her gorgeous eyes was something else.

"You're deathly afraid of horses," he said softly.

Meredith stared up into the sapphire eyes of the prince. The truth was she was not deathly afraid of horses.

But she was deathly afraid of a world out of her control.

The fact that he had got the *deathly afraid* part of her with such accuracy made her feel off balance, as if she was a wide open book to him.

She felt like she needed to slam that book shut, and quickly, before he read too much of it. Let him think she was afraid of horses!

It wasn't without truth, and it would be so much better than the full truth. That Meredith Whitmore was afraid of the caprice of life.

"Of course I'm afraid of horses," she said. "They are an uncommon occurrence in the streets of Wentworth. My closest encounter was at a Blossom Festival parade, where a huge beast went out of control, plunged into the crowd and knocked over spectators."

"You're from Wentworth, then?" he asked, still watching her way too closely.

He seemed more interested in that than her horse encounter. Well, good. That alone should erect the walls between them. "Yes," she said, tilting her chin proudly, "I am."

But instead of feeling as if the barrier went up higher, their stations in life now clearly defined, when he nodded slowly, she felt as if she had revealed way too much of herself! She turned from the prince swiftly, and clicked on the Play button on the screen, anxious to outrun the intensity in his eyes.

She focused, furiously, on the video. As the groom looked at his new wife, something melted in that young man's face. It was like watching a boy transform into a man, his look became so electric, so filled with tenderness.

Too aware of the prince standing beside her, Meredith scrambled to find sanctuary in the familiar.

"If you listen," she said, all business, all dance

instructor, "the music is changing, so are the steps. The dance has a more *salsa* feel to it now. Salsa originated in Cuba, though if you watch you'll see the influences are quite a unique blend of European and African."

"This really is your world, isn't it?" Kiernan commented.

"It is," she said, and she prayed to find refuge in it as she always had. It was just way too easy to feel something, especially as the dance they watched became more sensual. It felt as if the heat was being turned up in this room. Prince Kiernan was standing so close to her, she could feel the warmth radiating off his shoulder.

On the video, the young groom's whole posture changed, became sure and sexy, his stance possessive, as he guided his new bride around the room to the quickening tempo of the music.

"Here's another transition," Meredith said, "He's moving into a toned down hip-hop now, what I'd call a new school or street version rather than the original urban break dancing version."

A man's voice, an exquisite tenor soared above the dancing couple. *I never had a clue, until I met you, all that I could be—*

And the man let go of his wife's hand and waist and began to dance by himself. He danced as if his new bride alone watched him. Gone was the uncertain shuffle, and in its place was a performance that was nothing short of sizzling, every move choreographed to show a love story unfolding: passion, strength, devotion, a man growing more sure of himself with each passing second.

"You'll see this is very sporty," Meredith said, "and these kind of moves require amazing upper body strength, as well as flexibility and good balance.

It's part music, part dance, but mostly guts and pure athleticism."

She cast him a look. The prince certainly would have the upper body strength. And she had not a doubt about his guts and athleticism.

What she was doubting was her ability to keep any form of detachment while she worked with him trying to perfect such an intimate performance.

The dancer on the computer screen catapulted up onto one hand, froze there for a moment, came back down, and then did the very same move on his other side. He came up to his feet, tossed off his jacket, and loosened his tie.

"If he takes anything else off I'm leaving," Kiernan said. "It's like a striptease."

She shot him a look. Now this was unexpected. Prince Kiernan a prude? Where was the man of *Playboy Prince* fame?

They watched together as the groom's feet and hips and arms all moved in an amazing show of coordinated sensuality. The bride moved back to the edges of the crowd, who had gone wild. They were clapping, and calling their approval.

As the final notes of the music died the young groom took a run back toward his bride, fell to his knees and his momentum carried him a good ten feet across the floor. He caught his wife around her waist and gazed up at her with a look on his face that made Meredith want to melt.

The young groom's face mirrored the final words of the song, *I have found every treasure I ever looked for.*

There was something so astoundingly intimate about the video that in the stillness that followed, Meredith found herself almost embarrassed to look at Kiernan, as if they had seen something meant to be private between a man and a woman.

She pulled herself together. It was dancing. It was theater. There was nothing personal about it.

"What did you think?"

"I thought watching that was very uncomfortable," Kiernan bit out.

So, he'd picked up on the intimacy, too.

"It was like watching a mating dance," he continued.

"I see we have a bit of prudishness to overcome," she said, as if the discomfort was his alone.

But when his eyes went to her lips, Meredith had the feeling that the prince had a way of persuading her he was anything but a prude.

Something sizzled in the air between them, but she refused to allow him to see she was intimidated by it. And a little thrilled by it, too!

Meredith put her hands on her hips and studied him as if he was an interesting specimen who had found his way under her microscope.

"You didn't see the romance in it?" she demanded. "The delight of entering a new life? The hope for the future? His love for her? His willingness to do anything for her?"

"Up to and including making a fool of himself in front of—how many did you say—twelve million people? Every male in the world whose bride-to-be has insisted they look at this video is throwing darts at a target with his face on it!"

"He didn't look foolish! He looked enraptured. Every woman dreams of seeing *that* look on their beloved's face."

"Do they?" He was watching her again, with that look in his eyes. Too stripping, too knowing. "Do you?"

Did she? Did some little scrap of weakness still exist in her that wanted desperately to believe? That did want to see a look like the one on that young groom's face directed at her?

"I'm all done with romantic nonsense," she said, not sure whom she was trying to convince. Prince Kiernan? Or herself?

"Are you?" he asked softly.

"Yes!" Before he asked *why*, before those sapphire eyes pierced the darkest secrets of a broken heart, she rushed on.

"Prince Kiernan, the truth is I am an exception to the rule. People generally *love* romantic nonsense. Romance is the ultimate in entertainment," Meredith continued. "It has that feel-good quality to it, it promises a happy ending."

"Which it doesn't always deliver," he said sourly.

The ugly parts of his life had been splashed all over the papers for everyone to read about. He was, after all, Prince Heartbreaker.

But Meredith was stunned that what she felt for him, in that moment, was sympathy. For a moment, there was an unguarded pain in his eyes that made him an open book to her.

Which was the last thing she needed.

"All I'm saying," Meredith said, a little more gently, "is that if you can do a dance somewhat similar to that, it will bring down the house. What do you think?"

"How about I'm not doing anything similar to that? Not even if the entertainment value is unquestionable."

"Well, of course not that dance precisely, but that

video captures the spirit of what we want to do with this portion of the dance piece."

"It's too personal," he said firmly.

"It's for a dream sequence, Your Highness. This kind of dancing is very much like acting."

"Could we *act* more reserved?"

"I suppose we could. But where's the fun in that? And the delicious surprise? You know, you do have a reputation of being somewhat, um, stodgy. This would turn that on its head."

"Stodgy?" he sputtered. "Stern, remote, unapproachable, even snobby I can handle. But stodgy? Isn't stodgy just another word for prudish?"

He looked at her lips again, and again his eyes were an open book to her.

Meredith had to keep herself from gasping at what she saw there, something primitive in its intensity, a desire to tangle his hands in her hair, yank her to him, and find out who was really the prude, who was really stodgy.

But he shoved his hands deep in his pockets, instead.

Was she relieved? Or disappointed by his control?

Relieved, she told herself, but it sounded like a lie even in her own mind.

"We'll modify the routine to your comfort level," she said. "Now, let's just see where you're at right now. We can try and tweak the routine after that."

She turned her back to him, gathering herself, trying to regain her sense of professionalism. She fiddled with her equipment and the "bridal waltz" came on again.

She turned back to him and held out her hand. "Your Highness?"

It was the moment of truth. She had a sudden sense,

almost of premonition. If he accepted the invitation of her hand *everything* was going to change.

He must have felt it, too, because he hesitated.

Meredith took a deep breath.

"Your Highness?"

He took her hand.

And Meredith felt the sizzle of it all the way to her elbow.

CHAPTER THREE

"THIS IS HOW WE WOULD open the number," Meredith said, "with a simple three-step waltz, just like the one in the video."

Prince Kiernan moved forward, trying not to think of how her hand fit so perfectly into his, or about the softness of her delicately curved waist.

He was also trying not to look at her lips! The temptation to show Miss Meredith Whitmore he was no prude, and not stodgy, either, was overwhelming. And since he didn't appear to be convincing her with his stellar dance moves, her lips were becoming more a temptation by the minute.

"Hmm," she said, "Not bad *exactly*. I mean obviously you know a simple three-step waltz. You just aren't, how can I say this? Fluid! Mind you, that might just work at the beginning of the number. It would be great to start off with a certain stand-offishness, an armor that protects you from your discomfort with closeness."

Was she talking about the theatrics of the damned dance or could she seriously read his personality that well from a few steps? The urge to either kiss her or bolt strengthened.

He couldn't kiss her. It would be entirely inappropriate, even if it was to make a point.

And he didn't have to bolt. He was the prince. He could just say he'd changed his mind, bow out of his participation in the dance.

"But right here," she said, cocking her head at the music, "listen for the transition, we could have you loosen up. Maybe we could try that now."

Instead of saying he'd changed his mind, he subtly rolled his shoulders and loosened his grip on her hand. He wasn't quite sure what to do with the hand on her waist, so he flexed his fingers slightly.

"Prince Kiernan, this isn't a military march."

Oh, there were definitely shades of Dragon-heart in that tone!

He tried again. He used the same method he would use before trying to take a difficult shot with the rifle. He took a deep breath, held it, let it out slowly.

"No, that's tighter. I can feel the tension in your hand. Think of something you enjoy doing that makes you feel relaxed. What would that be?"

"Reading a book?"

She sighed as if it was just beginning to occur to her he might, indeed, be her first hopeless case. "Maybe something a bit more physical that you feel relaxed doing."

He thought of nothing he could offer—everything he could think of that he did that was physical required control, a certain wide-awake awareness that was not exactly relaxing, though it was not unenjoyable.

"Riding a bicycle!" she suggested enthusiastically. "Yes, picture that, riding your bike down a quiet tree-lined country lane with thatched roofed cottages and black-and-white cows munching grass in fields, your picnic lunch in your basket."

He changed his grip on her hand. If he wasn't mistaken

his palm was beginning to sweat, he was trying so hard to relax.

She glanced up at him, reading his silence. "Picnic lunch in the basket of a bicycle is not part of your world, is it?"

"Not really. I'm relaxed on horseback. But then that's not part of your world."

"And," she reminded him, a touch crankily, "horses are the reason why you're in this position in the first place."

Again, he felt that odd little shiver about being spoken to like that. It could have been seen as insolent.

But it wasn't. Adrian had warned him, after all. But what he couldn't have warned him was that he would find it somewhat refreshing to have someone just state their opinion so honestly to him, to speak to him so directly.

"In the pictures of you in the paper," she went on, "your horses seem absolutely terrifying—wild-eyed and frothy-mouthed." She shuddered.

"Don't be fooled by the pictures you see in the papers," he said. "The press delights in catching me at the worst possible moments. It helps with the villain-of-the-week theme they have going."

"I think it's 'villain-of-the-month'," she said.

"Or the year."

And unexpectedly they enjoyed a little chuckle together.

"So, you've seriously never ridden a bike?"

"Oh, sure, I have, but it's not a favorite pastime. I was probably on my first pony about the same time most children are given their first bicycles. Am I missing something extraordinary?"

"Not extraordinary, but so *normal*. The wind in your

hair, the exhilaration of sweeping down a big hill, racing through puddles. I just can't imagine anyone not having those lovely garden variety experiences."

He was taken aback by the genuine sympathy in her tone. "You feel sorry for me because I've rarely ridden a bike down a country lane? And never with a picnic lunch in the basket?"

"I didn't say I felt sorry for you!"

"I can hear it in your voice."

"Okay," she admitted, "I feel sorry for you."

"Well, don't," he snapped. "Nobody ever has before, and I don't see that it should start now. I occupy a place of unusual privilege and power. I am not a man who inspires sympathy, nor one who wants it, either."

"There's no need to be so touchy. It just struck me as sad. And it occurred to me that if you've never done that, you've probably never played in a mud puddle and felt the exquisite pleasure of mud squishing between your toes. You've probably never had a few drinks and thrown some darts. You've probably never known the absolute anticipation of having to save your money for a Triple Widgie Hot Fudge Sundae from Lawrence's."

"I fail to see your point."

"It's no wonder you can't dance! You've missed almost everything that's important. But what's to feel sorry about?"

He was silent. Finally, he said, "I didn't know my life had been so bereft."

She shrugged. "Somebody had to tell you."

And then he chuckled. And so did she. He realized she had succeeded in making just a little of the tension leave him. But at the same time, they had just shared something that took a little brick out of the wall of both their defenses.

"Well," he said dryly. "Imagine doing a bike ride with an entourage of security people, and members of the press jumping out in front of you to get that perfect picture. Kind of takes the country lane serenity out of the picture, doesn't it?"

"The peaceful feeling is leaving me," she admitted. "Is it a hard way to live?"

"I don't have a hard life," he said. "The opposite is probably true. Everyone envies me. And this lifestyle."

"That's not what I asked," she said quietly. "I wondered about the price, of not knowing if people like you for you or your title, of having to be on guard against the wrong photo being taken, the wrong word being uttered."

For an astounding moment it felt as if she had invaded very private territory. It annoyed him that the one brick coming out of the wall seemed to be paving the way for its total collapse.

For a moment he glimpsed something about himself being reflected back in her eyes.

He was alone. And she knew it. She saw what others had not seen.

He reminded himself that he *liked* being alone.

He allowed the moment to pass and instead of telling her anything remotely personal, he said, "How about fly-fishing a quiet stream? For my relaxing thing that I think about?"

Ah, he was shoving bricks back in the wall. Thank goodness!

"Perfect," she said. The perfect picture. Impersonal. "That kind of fishing even has a rhythm, doesn't it? See? Hold that picture in your head, because the way you are moving right now is much better."

Of course the minute she said that, it wasn't!

"I've fished on occasion," she said. "Nothing as fancy as fly-fishing. A pole and a bobber on a placid pond on a hot day."

"Really? I've always found women make scenes when they catch fish."

She rapped him with sharp playfulness on his shoulder. He was so startled by the familiarity of the move he stumbled.

"What a terrible stereotype," she reprimanded him. "I can't stand that fragile, helpless, squeals-at-a-fish stereotype."

"So, you're not a squealer?" he said, something like a smile grazing his lips.

She blushed, and it was her turn to stumble. "Good God, I didn't mean it like that."

He studied her face, and his smile deepened with satisfaction. He drew her closer and whispered in her ear, "Now who's the prude?"

But he didn't quite pull it off. Because she was blushing. He was blushing. And suddenly a very different kind of tension hissed in the air between them. He narrowly missed her toe.

With a sigh, she let go of him, moved a few steps away, regarded him thoughtfully.

"Adrian, I mean Prince Adrian, did not have these kinds of inhibitions."

"Adrian could use a few inhibitions in my opinion."

She sighed again. She was exasperated already and they'd been at this for all of fifteen minutes. "Are you going to be difficult every step of the way, Your Highness?"

"I'm afraid so."

"I'm up for a challenge," she told him stubbornly.

"I'm afraid of that, too." He said it lightly, but he was aware he was not kidding. Not even a little bit.

Meredith marshaled herself.

"Okay, let's start again." She moved closer to him, held up her hand. He took it.

"Deep breath, slide your foot, forward, one, two, right, one, two...slide, Your Highness, not goose-step! Look right into my eyes, not at your feet. Ouch!"

"That won't happen if I look at my feet," he said darkly.

"It's an occupational hazard. Don't worry about my feet. Or yours. Look into my eyes. Not like that! I feel as if you're looking at something unpleasant that got stuck to your shoe."

He scowled.

"And now as if you are looking at a badly behaved hound."

He tried to neutralize his expression.

"Bored, reviewing the troops," she pronounced.

"I am not bored when I'm reviewing the troops!"

She sighed. "Your Highness?"

"Yes?"

"Pretend you love me."

"Oh, boy," he muttered under his breath.

"Ouch," she said as her foot crunched under his toe. Well, it wasn't really his fault. What a shocking thing to say to a prince.

Pretend you love me.

Oh, God, what had made her say that? As if the tension in the air between them wasn't palpable enough!

Thankfully, the prince had no gift for pretense. He was glaring at her with a kind of pained intensity, as if she was posed over him with a dentist's drill. It was making her want to laugh, but not a happy laugh.

The nervous laugh of one who might just have to admit defeat.

Meredith had never met anyone she couldn't teach to dance. But then, of course, anyone who showed up at her studio *wanted* to learn.

And the truth?

She'd never been quite so intimidated before.

And not solely by the fact that Kiernan was a prince, either.

It was that he was the most masculine of men. He oozed a certain potent male energy that made her feel exquisitely, helplessly feminine in his presence. Her skin was practically vibrating with awareness of him, and she was on guard trying to hide that. Twice she had caught him staring at her lips with enough heat to sizzle a steak!

Unfortunately her job was to unleash all that potent male energy, to harness the surprising but undeniable chemistry between them, so that it showed in dance form. If she could manage that, she knew her prediction—that he would bring down the house—was entirely correct.

But Kiernan seemed as invested in keeping control as she was in breaking through it to that indefinable something that lurked beneath the surface of control.

"Maybe that's enough for the first day," she conceded after another painful half hour of trying to get him to relax while waltzing.

He broke his death grip on her hand with relief that was all too obvious.

"Same time tomorrow," she said, packing her gear. "I think we'll forget the waltz, and work on the next section tomorrow. I think you may find you like it. Some of the moves are amazingly athletic."

He didn't look even remotely convinced.

And an hour into their session the next morning neither was she!

"Your Highness! You have to move your hips! Just a smidgen! Please!"

"My hips are moving!"

"In lock step!"

Prince Kiernan glared at her.

Meredith sighed. "You want them to move more like this." She demonstrated, exaggerating the movement she wanted, a touch of a Tahitian fire dance. She turned and looked back at him.

The smoldering look she had wanted to see in his eyes while they were dancing yesterday was in them now.

It fell solidly into *the be careful what you wish for* category.

"Your turn," she said briskly. "Try it. I want to practically hear those hips *swishing.*"

"Enough," he said, folding his arms over the solidness of his chest. "I've had enough."

"But—

"No. Not one more word from you, Miss Whitmore."

His expression was formidable. And his tone left absolutely no doubt who the prince was.

Prince Kiernan was a beautifully made man, perfectly proportioned, long legs, flat hips and stomach, enormously broad shoulders.

But the way he moved!

"I'm just trying to say that while your bearing is very proud and military, it's a terrible posture for dancing!"

"I said not one more word. What part of that don't you

understand?" His tone was warning. "I need a break. And so do you."

He turned his back on her, took a cell phone from his pocket and made a call.

She stared at his broad back, fuming, but the truth was she was intimidated enough not to interrupt him.

When he turned back from his call, his face was set in lines that reminded her he would command this entire nation one day. He already shouldered responsibility for much of it.

"Come with me," he said.

Don't go anywhere with him, a voice inside her protested. It told her to stand her ground. It told her she had only days left to teach him to dance! They had no time to waste. Not a single second.

But Prince Kiernan expected to be obeyed and there was something in his tone that did not brook argument.

Meredith was ridiculously relieved that he didn't seem to need a break from *her*, only from dancing. He had already turned and walked away from her, holding open the ballroom door.

And Meredith was shocked to find herself passing meekly through it, actually anticipating seeing some of his palace home. She had always entered the palace grounds, and the ballroom directly through service entrances.

He went down the hallway with every expectation that she would follow him.

She ordered herself to rebel. To say that one more word that he had ordered her not to say.

But for what purpose? Why not follow him? Things were going badly. They certainly couldn't get any worse.

They hadn't even shared a chuckle this morning. Everything was way too grim, and he was way too uptight. Except for the *warrior about to ravish maiden* look she'd received after demonstrating how hips were supposed to move, the prince's guard was way up!

As it turned out, all she saw of the interior was that hallway. Still, it was luxurious: Italian marble floors, vases spilling over with fresh flowers set in recessed alcoves, light flooding in from arched windows, a painting she recognized, awed, as an original Monet. She had a cheap reproduction of that same painting in her own humble apartment.

The prince led her out a double French-paned glass door to a courtyard, and despite the freshness of the insult of being ordered not to say another word, something in Meredith sighed with delight.

The courtyard was exquisite, a walled paradise of ancient stone walls, vines climbing them. A lion's head set deep in one wall burbled out a stream of clear water. Butterflies glided in and out of early spring blooms and the warm spring air was perfumed with lilacs.

A small wrought iron table set with fine white linen was ready for tea. It was laid out for two, with cut hydrangeas as a centerpiece. A side table held a crystal pitcher, beaded with condensation from the chilled lemonade inside it. A three-tiered platter, silver, held a treasure trove of delicate pastries.

"Did you order this?" she asked, astounded. She barely refrained from adding *for me?* She felt stunned by the loveliness of it, and aware she felt her guard was being stormed.

As an only child she had dreamed tea parties, acted them out with her broken crockery, castoffs from houses her mother had cleaned. Only her companion then had been a favorite teddy bear, Beardly, ink stained by some disdainful rich child who'd had so many teddy bears to choose from that this vandalized one had made its way to the cleaning lady's daughter.

This time her companion was not nearly so sympathetic or safe!

"Sit down," he told her. Not an invitation.

The delight of the garden, and the table set for tea, had stolen her ability to protest. She sat. So did he. He poured lemonade in crystal goblets.

She took a tentative sip, and bit back a comment that it was fresh, not powder. As if he would know that lemonade could be made from a pouch!

"Have a pastry," he said.

Pride wanted to make her refuse the delicacies presented to her, but the deprived child she'd been eyed the plate greedily, and coveted a taste of every single treat on it. In her childhood she had had to pretend soda crackers and margarine were tea pastries. She selected a cream puff that looked like a swan. She wanted to look at it longer, appreciate the effort and the art that went into it.

And at the same time she did not want to let on how overawed she was. She took a delicate bite.

She was pretty sure Prince Kiernan had deliberately waited until she was under its influence before he spoke.

"Now," he said sternly, "we will discuss *swishing*."

The cream puff completely undermined her defenses, because she said nothing at all. She made no defense for swishing. None. In fact, she licked a little dollop of pure white cream off the swan's icing-sugar-dusted feathers.

For a moment, he seemed distracted, then he blinked and looked away.

But there was less sternness in his tone when he spoke.

"I am not swishing my hips," he told her. "Not today, not tomorrow, not ever."

The sting was taken out of it completely by the fact he glanced back at her just as she was using her tongue to capture a stray piece of whipped cream from her lips and seemed to lose his train of thought entirely.

"I think," she said reverently, "that's about the best thing I've ever tasted. Sorry. What were you saying?"

He passed the tray to her again. "I don't remember."

She was sure a more sophisticated person would be content with the cream puff, but the little girl in her who had eaten soda crackers howled inwardly at her attempt to be disciplined.

She mollified her inner child by choosing a little confection of chocolate and flaky pastry. He was doing this on purpose. Using the exquisiteness of the treats to bribe her, to sway her into seeing things his way.

"It was something about swishing," she decided. The pastry was so fragile it threatened to disintegrate under her touch. She bit it in half, closed her eyes, and suppressed a moan.

"Was it?" he growled, the sound of a man tormented.

"I think it was." She opened her eyes, licked the edge of the pastry, and a place where chocolate had melted on her hand. "That was fantastic. You have to try that one."

He grabbed the chocolate confection in question and

chomped on it with much less finesse than she would have expected from a prince. He seemed rattled.

"Do these have drugs in them?" she asked.

"I was just about to ask myself the same thing. Because I can't seem to keep my mind on—"

"Swishing," she filled in for him, eyeing the tray. "Never mind. It's not as important as I thought. We'll figure out something you're comfortable with."

He smiled, at first she thought because he had been granted reprieve from swishing. Then she realized he was smiling at her. "You have a sweet tooth. One wouldn't know to look at you."

Between his smile and the confections, and the fact he *looked* at her, she didn't have a chance.

"Yes," Meredith conceded, "let's forget swishing. It would have been fun. There's no doubt about that. The audience would have gone wild, but it's not really *you* if you know what I mean."

"Why don't you try that one?"

He was rewarding her for the fact he had gotten his way. She could not allow herself to be bribed. "Which one?"

"The one you are staring at."

"I couldn't possibly," she said wistfully.

"I'd be disappointed if you didn't."

"In that case," she said blissfully and took the tiny chocolate-dipped cherry from the tray. "Do you eat like this every day?"

"No," he said a trifle hoarsely, "I must say I don't."

"A pity."

Outside the delightful cloister of the garden, she heard the distinctive clop of hooves on cobblestone.

"Ah," he said with a bit too much eagerness, getting

up. "There's my ride. Please feel free to stay and enjoy the garden as long as you like. Tomorrow, then."

Again, it was not a suggestion or a question. No, she had just been given a royal dictate. He was done dancing for the day, whether she was or not.

He strode away from her, opened an arched doorway of heavy wood embedded in the rock wall and went out it.

Do something, Meredith commanded herself. So she did. She took a butter tart and popped the entire thing in her mouth. Then, ashamed of her lack of spunk, she leapt from her chair and followed him out the gate. She had to let the prince know that time was of the essence now. If he rode today they would have to work harder tomorrow. She'd made one concession, but she couldn't allow him to think that made her a pushover, a weakling so bowled over by his smile and tea in the garden that he could get away with anything.

She burst out of the small courtyard and found herself in the front courtyard of the castle. She stood there for a moment, delighted and shocked by the opulence of the main entrance courtyard in front of the palace.

The fountain at its center shot geysers of water over the life-size bronze of Prince Kiernan's grandfather riding a rearing warhorse. The courtyard was fragrant, edged as it was with formal gardens that were bright with exotic flowering trees.

The palace sat on top of Chatam's most prominent hill, and overlooked the gently rolling countryside of the island. In the near distance were farms and red-roofed farmhouses, freshly sown fields and lush pastures being grazed by ewes and newborn lambs.

In the far distance was the gray silhouette of the city of Chatam, nestled in the curves of the valley. Beyond that was the endless expanse of the sea.

Ancient oaks dappled the long driveway that curved up the hill to the palace with shade. At the bottom of that drive was a closed wrought iron and stone gate that guarded the palace entrance. To the left side of the gate was a tasteful stone sign, with bronze cursive letters, *Chatam Palace*, on the right, an enormous bed of roses, not yet in bloom.

Finding herself here, on this side of the gates, with the massive stone walls and turrets of the castle rising up behind her, was like being in a dream but Meredith tried to remind herself of the task at hand. She had to make her expectations for the rest of this week's practice sessions crystal-clear.

In front of the fountain, a groomsman in a palace stable uniform held a horse. Prince Kiernan had his back to her, his hand stroking one of those powerful shoulders as he took the reins from the groomsman and lifted a foot to the stirrup.

Meredith was not sure she had ever seen a man more in his element. The prince radiated the power, confidence and grace she had yet to see from him on the dance floor.

He looked like a man who owned the earth, and who was sure of his place in it.

The horse was magnificent. It was not one of the frightening horses she had seen in pictures, of that she was almost positive. Though large, and as shiny black as Lucifer, the horse stood quietly, and when he sensed her come out the gate he turned a gentle eye to her.

Except for nearly being trampled by that runaway

at the Blossom Festival parade all those years ago, Meredith had never been this close to a horse.

Instead of her planned lecture, she heard an awed *ooh* escape her lips.

Prince Kiernan glanced over his shoulder when he heard the small sound behind him.

And she, the one he thought he had successfully escaped, the one who could make eating a pastry look like something out of an X-rated film, stood there with round eyes and her mouth forming a little O.

He could leap on the horse and gallop away in a flurry of masculine showmanship. But there was something about the look on her face that stopped him.

He remembered she was afraid of horses.

He slipped his foot back out of the stirrup, and regarded Meredith Whitmore thoughtfully.

"Come say hello to Ben," he suggested quietly, dismissing his groomsman with a nod.

The debate raged in her face. Well, who could blame her? They had already crossed some sort of invisible line by having tea together. She was obviously debating the etiquette of the situation, wanting to be strictly professional.

And after watching her eat, he could certainly see the wisdom in that!

But he was aware of finding her reaction to the impromptu tea in the garden refreshing.

And he was aware of not being quite ready to gallop away.

And so what was the harm in having her meet his horse? He could tell she didn't want to, and that at the same time it was proving as irresistible to her as the crumpets had been. She moved forward as if she was being pulled on an invisible string. He could see her pulse racing in the hollow of her throat.

"Don't be afraid," Kiernan said.

She stopped well short of the horse. "He's gigantic," she whispered.

Prince Kiernan reached out, took her hand and tugged her closer.

They had been touching while they danced, but this was different. Everything about her was going to seem different after the semi-erotic experience of watching her devour teatime treats.

Still, he did not let her go, but pulled her closer, and then guiding her, he held her hand out to the horse.

"He wants to get your scent," he told her quietly.

The horse leaned his head toward her, flared his nostrils as he drew a deep breath, then breathed a puff of warm, moist air onto her hand where it was cupped in Kiernan's.

"Oh," she breathed, her eyes round and wide, a delighted smile tickling her lips. "Oh!"

"Touch him," Kiernan suggested. "Right there, between his mouth and his nose."

Tentatively, she touched, then closed her eyes, much as she had done when she decapitated the pastry swan with her lovely white teeth.

"It's exquisite," she said, savoring. "Like velvet, only softer."

"See? There's nothing to be afraid of."

But there was. And they both knew it.

She drew her hand away quickly from the horse's nose, and then out of the protection of Kiernan's cupped palm.

"Thank you," she said, and then rapidly, "I have to go."

He knew that was true, but he heard, not the words, but the fear, and frowned at it. The place where her heartbeat pulsed in her throat had gone crazy.

"Not yet," he said.

There was something in him that would not be refused. It went deeper than the station he had been born to, it went deeper than the fact he spoke and people listened.

There was something in him—a man prepared to lay down his life to protect those physically weaker than him—that challenged him to conquer her fear.

"Touch him here," he suggested, and ran his hand over the powerful shoulder muscle under the fringe of Ben's silky black mane.

She glanced toward the gate, but then made a choice. Hesitantly Meredith laid her hand where Kiernan's had been.

"I can feel his strength," she whispered, "the pure power of him."

Kiernan looked at where her hand lay just below the horse's wither, and felt a shattering urge to move her hand to his own chest, to see if she would feel his power, too, his strength.

Insane thoughts, quickly crushed. How was he supposed to dance with her if he followed this train of thought? And yet still, he did not let her go.

"If you put your nose to that place you just touched, you will smell a scent so sweet you will wonder how you lived without knowing it."

"I hope I'm not allergic," she said, trying for a light note, he suspected, desperately trying to break out of the spell that was being cast around them. But it didn't work. Meredith moved close to the horse, stood on tiptoe and drew in a deep breath.

She turned back to the prince, and he smiled with satisfaction at the transparent look of joyous discovery on her face.

"I told you," he said. "Do you want to sit on him?"

"No!" But the fear was gone. He saw her refusal, not as fright, but as an effort to fight the magic that was deepening around them.

"It's not dangerous," Kiernan said persuasively. "I promise I'll look after you."

He didn't know what he had said that was so wrong, but she suddenly went very still. The color drained from her face.

"Maybe another time," she said.

"You're trembling," Prince Kiernan said. "There's no need. There's nothing to be afraid of."

Meredith knew a different truth. There was so much to be afraid of people couldn't even imagine it.

But when she looked into Prince Kiernan's eyes, soft with unexpected concern, it felt as if the fear was taken from her. Which was ridiculous. The fact that she was inclined to trust him should make her feel more afraid, not less!

"Here, I'll help you up. Put your foot here, and your other hand here."

And she did. Even though she should have turned and run, she didn't. The temptation was too great to refuse.

She was a poor girl from Wentworth. And even though she had overcome her humble beginnings, she was still only a working woman.

This opportunity would never, ever come again.

To sit on a horse in the early spring sunshine on

the unspeakably gorgeous grounds of the Palace of Chatam.

With Prince Kiernan promising to protect her and keep her safe.

I promise I'll look after you. Those words were fair warning. She had heard those words, exactly those words, before.

When she had told Michael Morgan she was going to have his baby. And he had told her not to worry. He'd look after her. They would get married.

She could see the girl she had been standing on the city hall steps, waiting, her baby just a tiny bulge under her sweater. Waiting for an hour and then two. Thinking something terrible must have happened. Michael must have been in an accident. He must be lying somewhere hurt. Dying.

Her mother, who had refused to attend the ceremony, had finally come when it was dark, when city hall was long closed, and collected Meredith, shivering, soaked from cold rain, from the steps.

That's where trust got you. It left you way too open to hurt.

But even knowing that, Meredith told herself it would be all right just to allow herself this moment.

She took Kiernan's instructions, put her foot in the stirrup and took the saddle with her other hand. Despite her dancer's litheness, Meredith felt as if she was scrambling to get on that horse's back. But then strong hands lifted her at the waist, gave her one final shove on her rump.

Despite how undignified that final shove was, she settled on the hard leather of the saddle with a sense of satisfaction.

For the first time—and probably the only time—in her life, Meredith was sitting on a horse.

"Should we go for a little stroll?"

She had come this far. To get off without really riding the horse seemed like it would be something of a shame. She nodded, grabbed the front of the saddle firmly.

With the reins in his hands, Kiernan moved to the front of the horse. Instead of taking her for a short loop around the fountain, or down the driveway to the closed main gate, he led the horse off the paved area and onto the grass that surrounded the palace.

The whole time, his voice soothing, he talked to her.

"That's it. Just relax. Think of yourself as a blanket floating over him." He glanced back at her. "That's good. You have really good balance, probably from the dancing. That's it exactly. Just relax and feel the rhythm of it. It goes side to side and then back and forth. Do you feel that?"

She nodded, delighting in the sensation, embracing the experience. She thought after a moment he would turn around and lead her back to the courtyard, but he didn't.

"You'll see the first of the three garden mazes on your left," he said. "I used to love trying to find my way out of it when I was a boy."

He amazed her by giving her a grand tour of parts of the palace grounds that were not open to the public. But even had they been, the public would never have known that was the place he rode his first pony, that was where he fell and broke his arm, that was the fountain he and Adrian had put dish detergent in.

With the sun streaming down around her, the scent of the horse tickling her nostrils, and Kiernan out in front of her, leading the horse with such easy confidence, glancing back at her to smile and encourage her, Meredith realized something.

Perhaps the scariest thing of all.

For the first time since the accident that had taken her baby six years ago, she felt the tiniest little niggle of something.

It was the most dangerous thing of all. It was happiness.

CHAPTER FOUR

WHEN KIERNAN GLANCED BACK at Meredith, he registered her delight. There was something about her that troubled him. She was too serious for one so young. Something he could not understand haunted the loveliness of the deep golds and greens of her eyes.

And yet looking at her now those ever-present shadows, the clouds, were completely gone from her eyes. It made her lovely in a way he could not have guessed. He turned away, focused on the path in front of him. Her radiance almost hurt.

"Oh," she said. "Kiernan! He's doing something!"

Kiernan turned to see the horse flicking his tail. He laughed at the expression on her face.

"Now, that's a *swish*," he said. "A bothersome fly, nothing more."

But some tension had come into her, and he was driven to get rid of it.

"On this whole matter of swishing," he said solemnly. "A hundred years ago I could have had you hauled off to the dungeon to straighten you out about who was the boss. Ten days of bread and water would have mended your ways."

He was rewarded with her laughter.

"And if it didn't, I could have added rats."

"Really, Kiernan," she laughed, "you've proven you can have your way for a pastry. Hold the rats."

Have his way? Having his way with her suddenly took on dangerous new meaning. He could practically feel her hair tangled in his hands, imagine what it would be to take the lushness of her lips with his own.

He risked a glance at her, and saw, guiltily, that her meaning had been innocent. He was entranced by her sunlit face, dancing with laughter.

Her laughter was a delicious sound, pure mountain water, gurgling over rock, everything he had hoped for when he had given in to a desire to chase the shadows from her eyes. More.

The laughter changed her. It *was* the sun coming out from behind clouds. Meredith went from being stern to playful, she went from being somewhat remote to eminently approachable, she went from being beautiful to being extraordinary.

He laughed, too, a reluctant chuckle at first, and then a real laugh. Their combined laughter rang off the ancient walls and suffused the day with a light it had not had before.

Kiernan knew it was the first time in a long, long time that he had laughed like this. It was as if his relationship with Tiffany had brought out something grim in him that he never quite put away.

But then the moment of exquisite lightness was over, and as he gazed up into the enjoyment on her face he realized that he was not fully prepared for what he saw there. Even though he had encouraged this moment, he did not feel ready for the bond of it. There was an utter openness between them that was astounding.

He felt like a man who had been set adrift on ice, who was nearly frozen, and who had suddenly glimpsed the promise of the warm golden light of a fire in the distance.

But his very longing made him feel weak. What had he been thinking? He needed to guard against moments like this, not encourage them.

Kiernan was not sure he had ever felt quite that vulnerable. Not riding a headstrong horse over slippery ground, not even when the press had decided to crucify him, first over Francine, ten times worse over the Tiffany affair.

He turned abruptly back toward the courtyard, but when they arrived, he stood gazing up at her, not wanting to help her off the horse.

To touch her now, with something in him so open, felt as if it guaranteed surrender. He was Adam leaning toward the apple; he was Sampson ignoring the scissors in Delilah's hand.

Hadn't Tiffany just taught him the treacherous unpredictability of human emotion?

Still, Meredith wasn't going to be able to get off that horse without his help.

"Bring that one leg over," he said gruffly, and then realized he hadn't been specific enough, because she brought her leg over but didn't twist and swing down into the stirrup, but sat on his horse, prettily side-saddle.

And then, without warning, she began to slide off.

And he had no choice but to reach out and catch her around her waist, and pull her to him to take the impact from her.

She stood there in the circle of his arms, her chin tilted back, looking into his face.

"Kiernan," she said softly, "I don't know how to thank you. That was a wonderful morning."

But that was the problem. The wonder of the morning

had encouraged this new form of familiarity. Barriers were down. She hadn't used his proper form of address.

She didn't even know she hadn't, she was so caught in the moment. And she never had to know how he had *liked* how his name had sounded coming off her lips.

But it was just one more barrier down, one more line of protection compromised. He should correct her. But he couldn't. He hated it that the moment seemed to be robbing him of his strength and his resolve, his sense of duty, his *knowing* what was right.

Aside from Adrian, who was this comfortable with him, there were few people in his world this able to be themselves around him, this able to bring out his sense of laughter.

Francine had. Tiffany never.

She did not back out of the circle of his arms, and he did not release her. The laughter was gone from her face. Completely. She swallowed hard.

The guard he had just put up felt as if it was going to crumple. *Completely.* And if it did, he would never, ever be able to build it back up as strong as it had been before, like a wall that had been weakened by a cannonball hit.

"Your Highness?"

Now, she remembered the correct form of address. Too late. Because now he longed to hear his name off her lips.

That's what he had to steel himself against.

"Yes?"

"Thank you for not letting me fall," she said.

But the truth? It felt as if they were falling, as if they were entering a land where neither of them had ever been, without knowing the language, without having a map.

"It's not if you fall that matters," he said quietly. "Everyone falls. It's how you get up that counts."

A part of him leaned toward her, wanting, almost desperately to explore what was happening between them. As if, in that new land he had glimpsed so briefly in her eyes, he would find not that he was lost.

But that he was found.

And that he was not alone on his journey.

Kiernan gave himself a mental shake. He couldn't allow himself to bask in that feeling that he had been *seen*, this morning, not as a prince, but for the man he really was. And he certainly couldn't allow her to see that her praise meant something to him.

Music suddenly spilled out an open window above them. She cocked her head toward it. "What on earth?' she asked. "What kind of magic is this?"

The whole morning had had that quality, of magic. Now, it seemed imperative that he deny the existence of such a thing.

"It's not magic!" he said, his tone suddenly curt. "The palace chamber quartet is practicing, that's all. It happens every Tuesday at precisely eleven o'clock."

He liked precise worlds. Predictable ones.

"Your Highness?"

He looked askance at her.

"Shall we?"

Of course he wasn't going to dance with her! He was too open to her, too aware of how the sun shone off her hair, of the light in her eyes, of the glossy puffiness of her lips. He had a horse that needed looking after. Her laughter and his had already made him feel quite vulnerable enough.

And yet this surprise invitation had that quality of delicious spontaneity to it that he found irresistible. Plus, to refuse might deepen her puzzlement, and if she studied the mystery long enough, would she figure it out?

That there was something about her he liked, and at the same time, he disliked liking it. Intensely.

But there was one other thing.

He had seen a light come on in her today. It still shone there, gently below the surface, chasing away a shadow he had realized had been ever-present until this morning.

He might want to protect himself.

But not enough to push her back into darkness.

And so he dropped the reins, uncharacteristically not caring if the horse bolted back to the stable. He felt like a warrior at war, not with her, but with himself. Wanting to see her light, but not at the expense of losing his power.

He felt as if he was walking straight toward his biggest foe. Because, of course, his biggest foe was the loss of control that she threatened in him.

Here was his chance to wrest it back, to take the challenge of her to the next level. He gazed down at her, and then took her hand, placed his other one on her waist.

There was something about the spontaneity of it, about the casualness of it, about the drift of the music over the spring garden, that did exactly what she had wanted all along.

Something in him *breathed*. He didn't feel rigid. Or stiff. He felt on fire. *A man who would prove he was in charge of himself.*

A man who could flirt with temptation and then just shrug it off and walk away.

A man who could see her light, and be pulled to it, and want it for her, but at the same time, not be a moth that would be pulled helplessly into the flame.

He danced her around the courtyard until she was breathless. Until she was his whole world. All he could see was the light in her. All he could feel was the sensuous touch of her fingertips resting ever so lightly on the place where his back met his hip. All that he could smell was her scent.

The last note of music spilled out the window, held, and then died. He became aware again of a world that was not Meredith. The horse stood, his head nodding, birds singing, sun shining, the scent of lilacs thick in the air.

Now, part two of the equation. He had danced with the temptation.

Walk away.

But she was finally looking at him with the approval a prince deserved. He steeled himself not to let it go straight to his head.

"That was fantastic," Meredith said softly.

"Thank you." With a certain chilly note, as if he didn't give a fig about her approval.

"I think you're ready to learn a few modern dance step moves tomorrow."

Tomorrow. He'd been so busy getting through the challenge of the moment that he'd managed to completely forget that.

There were more moments to this challenge. Many more.

Kiernan had known she would be that kind of girl.

The if you give an inch, she'll take a mile kind.

The kind where if you squeezed through one challenge she threw at you, by the skin of your teeth, only, another would be waiting. Harder.

And just to prove she had much harder challenges in

store for him, she stood on her tiptoes and brushed his cheek with her lips.

Then she stepped back from him, stunned.

But not as stunned as he was. That innocent touch of her lips on his cheek stirred a yearning in him that was devastating. Suddenly his whole life seemed to yawn ahead of him, filled to the brim with activities and obligations, but empty of the one thing that truly mattered.

It doesn't exist, he berated himself. He'd learned that, hadn't he?

For a moment, she looked so surprised at herself that he thought she might apologize. But then, she didn't. No, she crossed her arms over her chest, and met his gaze with challenge, daring him to say something, daring him to tell her how inappropriate it was to kiss a prince.

But he couldn't. And therein was the problem. She was challenging his ability to be in perfect control at all times, and he hated that.

Resisting an impulse to touch the place on his cheek that still tingled from the caress of her soft lips, Kiernan turned from her, and went to his horse. He put his leg in the stirrup and vaulted up onto Ben's back. Without looking back, he pressed the horse into a gallop, took a low stone wall, and raced away.

But even without looking, he knew she had watched him. And knew that he had wanted her to watch him and be impressed with his prowess.

Some kind of dance had begun between them. And it had nothing at all to do with the performance they would give at *An Evening to Remember.*

On the drive home from the palace, Meredith replayed her audacity. She'd kissed the prince!

"It wasn't really a kiss," she told herself firmly. "More like a buss. Yes, a buss."

Somehow she had needed to thank him for all the experiences he had given her that day.

"So," she asked herself, "what's wrong with thank you?"

Still, if she had it to do again? She would do the same thing. She could not regret touching her lips to the skin of his cheek, feeling the hint of rough stubble beneath the tenderness of her lips, standing back to see something flash through his eyes before it had been quickly veiled.

She parked her tiny car in the laneway behind her apartment, a walk-up located above her dance studio in Chatam. She owned the building as a result of an insurance settlement. The building, and No Princes, had been her only uses for the money.

Both things had given her a little bit of motivation to keep going on those dark days when it felt like she could live no more.

Tonight, when she opened the door to the apartment that had given her both solace and sanctuary, she was taken aback by how fresh her wounds suddenly felt.

It had been six years since it had happened.

A grandmother who had just picked up her granddaughter from day care walking a stroller across a street. Who could know why Meredith's mother, Millicent, had not heard the sirens? Tired from working so hard? Mulling over the dreams that had been shattered? A stolen vehicle the police were chasing went through the crosswalk. Meredith's mother, Millicent, had died at the scene, after valiantly throwing her body in front of the stroller. Carly had succumbed to her

injuries a few days later, God deaf to the pleas and
prayers of Meredith.

Now, the apartment seemed extra empty and quiet
tonight, no doubt because today, for the first time in so
long, Meredith had allowed herself to feel connected to
another human being.

Meredith set her bag inside the door, and went straight
to the bookshelf, where there were so many pictures of
her baby, Carly. She chose her favorite, took it to the
couch, and traced the lines of her daughter's chubby
cheeks with her fingertips.

With tears sliding down her cheeks, she fell asleep.

When she awoke she was clutching the photo to her
breast. But instead of feeling the sadness she always
felt when she awoke with a photo of her daughter, she
remembered the laughter, and the happiness she had felt
today.

And felt oddly guilty. How could she? She was
not ready to be happy again. Nor could she trust it.
Happiness came, and then when it went, as it inevitably
did, the emptiness was nearly unbearable.

Meredith considered herself strong. But not strong
enough to hope. Certainly not strong enough to sustain
more loss. She was not going to embrace the happiness
she had felt today. No, not at all. In fact, she was going
to steel herself against it.

But the next morning she was aware she was not
the only one who had steeled herself against what had
happened yesterday.

If Meredith thought they had made a breakthrough
yesterday when she had ridden the horse and Kiernan
had danced in the courtyard with her, she now saw she
was sadly mistaken.

He had arrived this morning in armor. And he danced

like it, too! Was the kiss what had done it? Or the whole day they had experienced together? No matter, he was as stiffly formal as though he had never placed his hand on her rump to sling her into the saddle of his horse, as if he had never walked in front of her, chatting about his childhood on the palace grounds.

Meredith tried to shrug her sense of loss at his aloofness away and focus on the job at hand.

She had put together a modified version of the newlyweds' dance from the internet and Prince Kiernan had reluctantly approved the routine for *An Evening to Remember.* She had hoped to have some startling, almost gymnastic, moves in it, which would show off the prince's amazing athletic ability.

But the prince, though quite capable of the moves, was resistant.

"Does the word *sexy* mean anything to you?"

Something burned through his eyes, a fire, but it was quickly snuffed. "I'm doing my best," he told her with cool reserve, not rattled in the least.

But he wasn't. Because she had glimpsed his best. This did not even seem like the same man she had danced with yesterday in the courtyard, so take-charge, so breathtakingly masculine, so sure.

The stern line of his lip was taking on a faintly rebellious downward curve. Pretty soon, he would announce *enough* and another day of practice would be lost.

Not that yesterday had been lost.

She sighed. "You know the steps. You know the rudiments of each move. But you're like a schoolboy reciting math tables by rote. Something in you holds back."

"That's my nature," he said. "I'm reserved. Something in me always holds back." His eyes fastened on her lips, just for a split second, and she felt her stomach do a loop-the-loop worthy of an acrobatic airplane.

If he didn't hold back, would he kiss her? What would his lips taste like? Feel like? Given her resolve to back away from all those delicious things she had felt yesterday, Meredith was shocked by how badly she wanted to know. She was shocked by the sudden temptation to throw herself at him and take those lips, to shock the sensuality out of him.

But she also needed for both of them to hold back if she was going to keep her professional distance. And she needed just as desperately for him to let go if she was going to feel professional pride in teaching him!

It was a quandary.

"Is it your nature to be reserved," she questioned him, "or your role in life?"

"In my case, those are inextricably intertwined."

He said that without apology.

"I understand that, but in dancing there is no holding back. You have to put everything into it, all that you were, all that you have been, all that you hope to be someday."

The question was, if he gave her all that, how was she going to walk away undamaged?

"This is a ten-minute performance at a fund-raiser," he reminded her, "not the final exam for getting into heaven."

But that's what she wanted him to experience, *exactly*. She realized for her it had become about more than their performance.

There was a place when you danced well, where you became part of something larger. It was an incredible feeling. It was a place where you rose above problems.

And tragedies. A place where you were free of your past and your heartaches. Yes, just like touching heaven.

But somehow she could not tell him that. It was too ambitious. He was right. It was a ten-minute performance for the fund-raiser opening of Blossom Week. Meredith was here to teach him a few dance steps, nothing more.

When had it become her quest to unlock him? To show him something of himself that he had never seen before? To want him to experience *that* feeling. Of heaven.

And that she was dying to see?

It had all become too personal. And she knew that. She had to get her own agenda straight in her head.

Teach him to do the routine, perform it well, and be satisfied if the final result was passable if not spectacular. The prince putting in a surprising appearance, making a game effort at the steps would be enough. The people of Chatam would *love* his performance, a chance to see him let his hair down, even if he was somewhat wooden.

Though, for her, to only accomplish a passable result would feel like a failure of monumental proportions. Especially since she had glimpsed yesterday what he could be.

Her eyes suddenly fell on two jackets that hung on pegs inside the coat check at the far end of the ballroom. They were the white jackets of the palace housekeeping staff.

As soon as she saw them, she knew exactly what she had to do.

And as she contemplated the audacity of her plan, she could have sworn she heard a baby laugh, as if it was *so* right.

It was a memory of laughter, nothing more, but she could see the face of the beautiful child who had been taken from her as clearly as though she still had the photo on her chest.

She was aware again, of something changing in her. Sweetly. Subtly. It wasn't that she wasn't sad. It was that the sadness was mixed with something else.

A great sense of gratitude for having known love so deeply and so completely.

Meredith was suddenly aware that her experience with love had to make her a better person.

It had to.

Her daughter's legacy to her had to be a beautiful one. That was all she had left to honor her with.

And if that meant taking a prince to a place where he was not so lonely and not so alone, even briefly, then that was what she had to do.

It wasn't about the dance they were doing at all.

It was about the kind of person she was going to choose to be.

And yes, it was going to take all her courage to choose it.

She moved past the prince to the coat check, plucked the jackets off the wall, and then turned back and took a deep breath.

Yesterday, spontaneity had brought them so much closer to the place they needed to be than all her carefully rehearsed plans and carefully choreographed dance steps.

Today, she hoped for magic.

CHAPTER FIVE

THE PRINCE BADLY WANTED his life back. He wanted *An Evening to Remember* to be over. He wanted the temptation of Meredith over; watching her demonstrate hip moves, taking her hand in his, touching her, looking at her and pretending to love her.

It was easily the most exhausting and challenging work he had ever done, and the performance couldn't come quickly enough in his opinion.

Though, somewhere in his mind, he acknowledged over would be over. No more rehearsals. No more bossy Meredith Whitmore. Who didn't respect his station, and was impertinent. Who was digging at him, trying to find the place in him he least wanted her to see, refusing to take no for an answer.

Who could make eating pastries look like an exercise in eroticism one minute, and look at a horse with the wide-eyed wonder of a child the next. Whose lips had felt like butterfly wings against his cheek.

Stop, Kiernan ordered himself.

She was aggravating. She was annoying. She was damnably sexy. But she was also *refreshing* in a way that was brand new to him. She was not afraid to tell him exactly what she thought, she was not afraid to make demands, she was not afraid of him, not awed by his station, not intimidated by his power.

And that, he reluctantly admitted, was what he was going to miss when it was all over. In so much of his life he was the master. What he said went. No questions. No arguments. No suggestions. No discussion.

How was it that in a dance instructor from Wentworth, he felt he had met his equal?

There was no doubt going to be a huge space in his life once she was gone. It seemed impossible she could have that kind of impact after only a few days. But he didn't plan to dwell on it.

Prince Kiernan was good at filling spaces in his life. He had more obligations than he had time, anyway, and many of those were stacking up as he frittered away hours and hours learning the dance routine he was coming to hate.

"We're going to go somewhere else today," Meredith announced, marching back over from the coat room with something stuffed under her arm. "I think the ballroom itself may be lending to the, er, stuffiness, we're experiencing. It's too big, too formal."

But he knew it wasn't the room she found stuffy. It was him.

"First stodgy, now stuffy," he muttered.

"Don't act insulted. You said yourself the role you play has made you that way."

"No, you suggested it was the role I played. I said I was born this way. And I never used the word stuffy. I think I said reserved."

"Okay, whatever," she said cheerfully. "We're going to do a little experiment today. With your reserve."

Oh-oh, this did not bode well for him. He was already hanging onto his control by the merest thread.

"Here," she said pleasantly, "put this on."

She handed him one of the white jackets she had stuffed under her arm. The one she handed him had the name *Andy* embroidered over one pocket in blue thread. He hesitated. What was the little minx up to?

Mischief. He could see it in the twinkle in her eye.

He should stop her before she got started, and he knew that. But despite the fact he had told himself he wasn't going to dwell on it, soon their time together would be over. Why not see what mischief she had planned? That spark in her eye was irresistible anyway, always reminding him that there was a shadow in her.

Like the unexpected delight of taking her for tea and then on that ride, this was part of the unexpected reprieve he'd been given from the stuffy stodginess of his life. He was aware he *wanted* to see what she had up her sleeve today.

So he slipped the white jacket over his shirt and did up the buttons. It was too tight across the chest, but she inspected him, and frowned. She went back to the coat check and reappeared with a white ball cap.

"There," she said, handing it to him. "Pull it low over your eyes. Perfect. All ready to smuggle you out of the palace." She shrugged into a white jacket of her own. It said *Molly* on the pocket.

"We can't smuggle me out of the palace," he said, but he was aware it was a token protest. Something in him was already taking wing, flying over the walls.

"Why not?"

"There are security concerns. I have responsibilities and obligations you can't even dream of. I can't just waltz out of here without letting anyone know where I'm going and why."

"To improve your waltz, I think you should. See?

There's that reserve again. Your Highness—no, make that Andy—have you ever broken the rules?"

"I don't have the luxury," he told her tightly.

She smiled at him. "Prince Kiernan of Chatam doesn't. Andy does. Let's go. It's just for a little while. Maybe an hour. In some ways, you're a prisoner of your life. Let's break out. Just this once."

He stood there for a moment, frozen. Again, he had a sense of her saying what no one else said.

And seeing what no one else saw.

She didn't see the prince. Not entirely. If she did, she would not have dared to touch his cheek with her lips yesterday. She saw a man first. The trappings of his status underwhelmed her. She saw straight through to the price he paid to be the prince.

And she wanted to rescue him. There was a kind of crazy courage in that that was as irresistible as the mischief in her eyes.

Of course he couldn't just go. It would be the most irresponsible thing he had ever done.

On the other hand, why not? The Isle of Chatam was easily the safest place in the world. He was supposed to be at dance class. No one would even miss him for a few hours.

Suddenly what she was offering him seemed as impossible to resist as the mischief that made her eyes spark more green than brown.

Freedom. Complete freedom, the one thing he had never ever known.

"Coming, Andy?" she said.

He sighed. "Molly, I hope you know what you're doing."

"Trust me," she said.

And Kiernan realized he was starting to. The one

thing he wanted to do least was trust a woman! And yet somehow she was wiggling her way past his defenses and entering that elite circle of people that he truly trusted.

He followed her outside to the staff parking lot. She led him to the tiniest car he had ever seen, a candy-apple-red Mini.

She got in, and he opened the passenger door and slid in beside her. His knees were in approximately the vicinity of his chin.

"They've gotten used to me at the service entrance," she said. "I'll just give them a wave and we'll breeze on through."

And that's exactly what happened.

In moments they were chugging along a narrow country road, he holding on for dear life. Kiernan had never ridden in a vehicle that was so…insubstantial. He felt as if they were inches above the ground, and as if every stone and bump on the road was jarring his bones. He actually hit his head on the roof of the tiny vehicle.

"Where are we going?" he asked.

"Remember I asked you about squishing mud up through your toes?"

"Yes, I do."

"That's where we're going."

"I don't want to squish mud up between my toes," he said, though he recognized his protest, once again, as being token. The moment they had driven through that back service gate to the palace something in him had opened.

He had made a decision to embrace whatever the day held.

"It doesn't matter if you want to or not. Andy does."

"But why does he?" he asked.

"Because he likes having *fun*."

"Oh, I see. There's nothing stuffy or stodgy about our man, Andy."

"Exactly," she said, and beamed at him with the delight of a teacher who had just helped a child solve a difficult problem. "Andy, you and I are about to give new meaning to *Dancing with Heaven*."

"I don't know the old meaning, Molly."

"You've never seen *Dancing with Heaven*? It's a movie. A classic romantic finding-your-true-self movie that has dance at its heart. It starred Kevin McConnell."

He didn't care for the dreamy way she said that name.

"I'll have to put watching *Dancing with Heaven* on your homework list."

"Andy doesn't like homework."

"That's true."

"He likes playing hooky. But when he's at school?"

"Yes?"

"He winks at the teacher and makes her blush."

"Oh-oh," she said.

"He likes motorcycles, and black leather, driving too fast, and breaking rules."

"My, my."

"He likes loud music and smoky bars, and girls in too-short skirts and low-cut tops who wiggle their hips when they dance."

"Oh, dear."

"He thumbs his nose at convention. He's cooled off in the town fountain on the Summer Day celebrations, disobeyed the Keep Off signs at Landers Rock, kept his hat on while they sing the national anthem."

"That's Andy, all right."

"He likes swimming in the sea. Naked. In the moon-light."

Unless he was mistaken, Meredith gulped a little before she said, "I've created a monster."

"You should be more careful who you run away with, Molly."

"I know."

"But they say every woman loves a bad boy."

Something in her face closed. She frowned at the road. Kiernan realized how very little he knew about her, which was strange because he felt as if he knew her deeply.

"Do you have a boyfriend?" He hadn't thought to ask her that before. There were no rings on her fingers, so he had assumed she was single. Now he wondered why he had assumed that, and wondered at why he was holding his breath waiting for her answer.

"I'm single." Her hands tightened on the wheel.

"I'm surprised." But ridiculously *relieved*. What was that about, since if ever there was a man sworn off love it was him? Why would he care about her marital status?

Only because, he assured himself, he didn't even want to think about her with a bad boy.

She hesitated, looked straight ahead. "I became preg-nant when I was sixteen. The father abandoned me. It has a way of souring a person on romance." He heard the hollowness in her voice, but he could hear something more.

Unbearable pain. And suddenly his concern for pro-tecting his own damaged heart evaporated.

"And the baby?" he asked quietly. Somehow he knew this woman could never have an abortion. Never.

And that adoption seemed unlikely, too. There was something about the fierce passion of that first dance he had witnessed her performing that let him know that. She would hold on to what she loved, no matter what the cost to her.

He glanced at her face. She was struggling for control. There was something she didn't want to tell him, and suddenly, with an intuition that surprised him, he knew it was about the shadow that he so often saw marring the light in her eyes.

He held his breath, again, wanting, no, *needing* to know that somehow she had come to trust him as much as he had come to trust her, even if it was with the same reluctance.

"It was a little girl. I kept her," she whispered. "Maybe a foolish thing to do. My mom and I had to work night and day cleaning houses to make ends meet. But I don't regret one second of it. Not one. All I regret is that I couldn't be with her more. With both of them more."

He felt a shiver go up and down his spine.

"My mom picked her up from day care for me on a particularly hectic day. They were crossing a street when a stolen car being chased by the police hit them."

Her voice was ragged with pain.

"I'm so sorry," he said, aware of how words were just not enough. "You seem much too young to have survived such a tragedy."

In a broken whisper she went on, "She wasn't even a year old yet."

Her shoulders were trembling. She refused to look at him, her eyes glued to the road.

He wanted to scream at her to pull over, because he needed to gather her in his arms and comfort her. But

from the look on her face there were some things there
was no comforting for.

"I'm so sorry," he said again, feeling horrible and
helpless. He reached out and patted her shoulder, but
she shrugged out from under his hand, her shoulder stiff
with pride.

"It's a long time ago," she said, with forced brightness. "Today, let's just be Molly and Andy, okay?"

It couldn't be *that* long ago. She wasn't old enough
for it to have been that long ago.

But she had trusted him with this piece of herself.

And her trust felt both fragile and precious. If he said
the wrong thing it felt like this precious thing she had
offered him would shatter.

Still, he could not quite let it go. He had to listen to
the voice inside him that said, *ask her.*

"Could you tell me their names? Your baby's and your
mother's?" he asked, softly, ever so softly. "Please?"

She was silent for so long that he thought she would
refuse this request. When she answered, he felt deeply
moved, as if she had handed him her heart.

"Carly," she whispered. "My baby's name was Carly.
My mother's was Millicent, but everyone called her
Millie."

"Carly," he said softly, feeling it on his tongue.
"Millie."

And then he nodded, knowing there was nothing else
to say, but holding those names to him like the sacred
trust that they were.

There was something about the way he said her daughter
and mother's names, with genuine sadness, and a simple
reverence, that gave Meredith an unexpected sense of
being comforted. Over the past days she had come to

know Prince Kiernan in a way that made it easy to forget he was still the most powerful man in the land.

Something about the way he uttered those names made her understand his power in ways she had not before. His speaking Carly's name was oddly like a blessing.

Meredith felt tears at his gentleness sting her eyes, but she did not let them flow. Kiernan reached out, and loosed her hand from the gearshift, and gave it a hard squeeze before letting it go.

Why had she told him about Carly? And her mother? She could have just as easily left it at she was single.

Was it because she was asking him to let his guard down? And that request required more of her, too? Was it because some part of her had trusted he would handle it in just the right way?

Whatever it was, she waited for a sense of vulnerability to come, a sense that she had revealed too much of herself.

But it did not. Instead, she felt an unexpected sense of a burden that she had carried alone being, not lifted, but shared.

A prince sharing your burden, she scoffed at herself, but her scorn did not change the way she felt, lighter, more open.

But for now, she reminded herself, a newfound sense of awe of Kiernan would not forward her goal. He needed to be taken off his pedestal if she ever hoped to get him to dance as if he meant it.

So for today, Kiernan was not a prince, not the most wealthy, most influential, most powerful man in Chatam. Today he would be just Andy. And she was not a woman with an unbearable sadness in her past, just *Molly*, two palace housekeeping workers playing hooky from work for the day.

They arrived at the small unmarked pullout, the trailhead for what Meredith considered one of the greatest treasures of the Isle of Chatam, Chatam Hot Springs.

Meredith opened the boot of her small car, and loaded "Andy" down with bags and baskets to carry up the steep trail that wound through the sweetly scented giant cedar woods. She was enjoying this charade already. She would have never asked a prince to carry her bags!

Meredith was relieved to see, as they came around the final twist in the trail, there was not a single soul at Chatam Hot Springs. The natural springs were a favorite local haunt, but not this early in the day and not midweek. She had taken a chance that the hot springs would be empty, and they were.

Kiernan set down his cargo and gazed around. "What a remarkable place."

Puffs of mist rose above the turquoise waters that filled a pool edged by slabs of flat black slate rocks. Freshwater falls cascaded down a mossy outcropping at the far end of the pool. Lush ferns, and bunches of grass, sown with tiny purple and blue wildflowers, surrounded the rocks and the pool.

"You've never been here?"

"I've heard of it, and seen photographs of it many times. But to come here? When the royal entourage arrives, security would necessitate closing it to the people who enjoy it most. I have so many other pleasures at my disposal that it would seem unduly selfish to want this one, also."

She was already vulnerable to him because somehow the way he had reacted to her history had been so quietly *right*. Now she saw that despite the fact he lived in a position that could have easily bred arrogance, it had not. Kiernan clearly saw his position not as one of absolute power, but one of absolute service.

Still, the time for being too serious today was over.

"Oh, Andy," she chided him. "You're talking as if you think you're royalty!"

Still, she was delighted he had never been here before, pleased that she was the one who had brought him to something new, beautiful and unexpected.

"Oh, Molly," he said contritely. "You know me. Delusions of grandeur."

"I have a plan for bringing you down a few notches, Andy."

"I can barely wait."

And it actually sounded as if he meant that, as if he was embracing this experience with an unexpected eagerness.

"Well, then, kick off your shoes, and roll up your pants," Meredith suggested. "This is what I want to show you."

He didn't even argue with her.

Hidden in a tiny glade beside the hot springs, separated from the main pool by a dripping curtain of thick foliage, was a dip in the ground, approximately a quarter the size of the ballroom, that was filled with oozing, gray mud.

Meredith waded in. "Careful, it's—" just as she tried to warn him, one of her feet slipped. But before she even fully registered she was falling, Kiernan was beside her. He wrapped his arm around her waist, took her arm, and steadied her.

"Oh, Molly, you're a clumsy one. I'd give up those dreams of being a dancer if I were you."

She felt as if she could not get enough of the playful tone in his voice.

"I'll give up my dancer dreams if you'll give up yours of being a prince."

"Done," he said, with such genuine relief they both laughed.

"It's warm," he said, astounded, apparently unaware that even though he had let go of her waist, he still held her arm. "I've never felt anything quite like this."

And neither had she. Oh, the mud was exquisite; warm and thick, it oozed up through her toes, and then around her feet, and ankles, up her calves, but it was his hand, still steadying her arm, which she had never felt anything like.

They had been touching each other for days now.

But, except for that magical moment when the music had spilled over the courtyard, their dancing together had been basically all business. Their barriers had both been so firmly up. But that kiss she had planted on his cheek had taken the first chink out of those barriers, and now there were more chinks falling.

And so this outing and this experience wasn't all business even if she had cloaked her motivation in accomplishing a goal.

Meredith looked at Kiernan's face, dappled with sunshine coming through the feathery cedars that surrounded the pool, and something sighed within her. His face was exquisite, handsome and perfect, but she had never seen the expression she saw on it now.

Prince Kiernan's eyes were closed. He looked completely relaxed, and something like contentment had crept into the normally guarded lines of his face. He tilted his chin to the sun, and took a deep breath, sighed it out.

It was good.

But it wasn't enough.

She wanted, *needed* to see with a desperation not totally motivated by her end goal, the prince lose his inhibitions, that *restraint*, that was like an ever-present palace guard, surrounding him. Keeping others away from him. But also keeping him away from others.

She let go of his hand. She stooped, and buried her own hand in the mud, closed her fist around an oozing gob of goo. For a moment she hesitated.

It was true. Kiernan was just way too restrained. He could never reach his potential as a dancer while he carried that shield around him.

But this was probably still just about the worst idea she had ever had. She lived in a land still ruled by a very traditional monarchy. Schoolchildren and soldiers started their day by swearing their allegiance and obedience to this man's mother, Queen Aleda. But in time it would be him they stood and pledged their hearts to.

He had already shouldered much of the mantle of responsibility. Meredith knew, partly from the newspapers, and confirmed by the phone calls he sometimes had to take during dance practice, his interest in the economic health of the island was keen, that he had sharp business acumen, and that some of his initiatives had improved the standard of living for many people who lived here.

He promoted Chatam tirelessly abroad. He headed charities. He sat on hospital boards. He was the commander-in-chief of the military.

This man who stood with her, his pants rolled up to his knees, had influence over the lives of every single person in Chatam.

Really, it was no wonder he had trouble relaxing! So, this was probably one of the worst ideas Meredith had ever had. She *was* too cheeky. You did not, after all, in a land ruled by a monarchy, pick up a handful of oozing soft mud and hurl it at your liege!

But Meredith was committed to her course. Knowing somehow, in her heart, not her head, this was, absurdly, wonderfully, the *right* thing, she let fly with a handful of mud.

It caught him in the chest, and he staggered back a step, startled. He opened his eyes and stared down at the mud bullet that had exploded on his shirt.

His reaction would tell her a great deal about this man.

Furious anger?

Remote silence?

Complete retreat?

But, no, a smile tickled his lips, and when he looked up at her, she felt she might weep for what she had unmasked in his eyes.

"Disrespectful wench," he said. "I'd swear you are looking for a few nights in the dungeon."

There was a delightful playfulness in his tone.

"Andy! Are you in your prince delusion again? Dungeons, for pity sake! I suppose you'll be telling me about bread and water and rats next. Poor you. Tut-tut."

"Prince delusion? Oh, no, not at all. I'm in my warrior delusion, and you have just called me to battle. But I'm going to warn you, all prisoners go to the dungeon. If you please me, I might spare you the rats."

She giggled, a trifle nervously, because something

smoked in his eyes when he talked of making her his prisoner.

What had she started? And could she really handle it?

Kiernan stooped and came up with his big hand full of mud. He squinted at her thoughtfully, drew back his arm and took aim.

She began to run an awkward zigzag pattern through the sucking mud. The dark sludge he hurled whisked by her head.

"Ha-ha," she called over her shoulder. Meredith ducked, picked up her own mud ball and flung it back at him. But he'd had time to rearm, too.

Their mud balls crossed paths with each other, midair. His hit her solidly on the arm, with a warm, soft splat. It was like being hit with a dollop of just-out-of-the-oven pudding. Her missile wobbled through the air and went straight for his head.

Despite the fact he raised his arm in defense against the slow-flying projectile, it exploded against his raised bicep, and particles of it landed on his cheek, blossoming there like the petals of a mud flower. She drew her breath, shocked by her own unintentional audacity.

"I'm so sorry!" she called.

"Not nearly as sorry as you're going to be," he warned her.

He stopped, carefully wiped the muck off his cheekbone, and glared at her with mock fierceness. But Meredith saw there was nothing mock about the fact he did now look like a warrior! Of the barbaric variety that painted their faces before they went to battle.

He let out a cry worthy of that warrior and came after

her, stooping and hucking mud as fast as he could fill his hands with it.

In moments the glade rang with his shouts and her playful shrieking. They threw mud back and forth until they were both covered in dark blotches, until their hair was lost under ropy dreadlocks of sludge, their hands were like mud mitts at their sides, and their clothes had disappeared under layers of smelly black goo. Finally, only his teeth and the whites of his eyes still looked white. Andy's shirt was probably beyond repair.

The glade filled with the sounds of their laughter and playful insults, the sounds of them gasping for breath as they struggled to run through the sucking mud to escape each other's attacks.

"Take that, Molly!"

"You missed! Andy, you throw like a girl."

"*You* missed. *You* throw like a girl."

"But I am a girl!"

"A girl? A mud monster, risen from the deep! Take that!"

They were laughing so hard they were choking on it. It rang off the rocks around them, rode on the mist.

Despite the noise, the chaos, the hilarity, something quiet blossomed in Meredith. Something she had felt, ever so briefly on that horse yesterday, but other than that not for a long, long time.

Joy.

The quiet awareness of it knocked her off balance. With Kiernan hot on her heels, his raised hand full of mud rockets, she slipped. She went down in slow motion, somehow managing to twist so she wouldn't go into the muck face first. The mud cushioned her fall, and she fell on her back with a sucking *splat*.

She watched as Kiernan, too close, tried desperately

to stop, but his arms windmilled, and he fell right on top of her, saving her from the worst of his weight by bracing his arms around her.

She stared up into the face of her warrior prince. His eyes were alight with laughter, looking bluer than she had ever seen them look. His smile, against the backdrop of his muddy face, was brilliant, white as snow against a stone.

She had never felt anything quite so exquisite. She rested in a bed of warm mud, her skin slippery and sensuous with it. And Kiernan, equally as slippery, held himself off of her, but there were places their bodies met. His hard lines were pressed into the soft curves of her legs and her hips.

She touched him every day. But his guard had always been up.

Hers had been, too.

Only something, delicate and subtle, had shifted between them.

The laughter died in the air around them, and was replaced with a silence so profound that it vibrated with a growing tension, a deep awareness of each other.

He stared down at her, and some unguarded tenderness crept into his muddy, warrior's face.

Still holding most of his weight off her with one arm, he touched her lip with the hand he had just freed, scraped gently with his thumb.

Her joy escalated into exhilaration at the exquisite sense of being touched in such an intimate place, in such an intimate way.

"You have mud right here," he whispered, by way of excuse, but his voice hoarse.

For a splendid moment it felt as if every barrier was

down between them. Every one. As if her world was as wide open as it had ever been.

Everything became remarkable: the song of a bird nearby, the feel of the mud cushioning her, the smells that tickled her nostrils, the green of the fern plumes behind him.

Where his legs were sprawled across hers, the slide of their skin together where it made slight contact at their hips, the amazing light in his sapphire eyes, the scrape of his thumb against her lip, the slick muddiness of his hair, the sensual curve of his lips.

He was so close to her she could see the dark beginning of stubble on his cheeks, and his chin. He was so close to her his breath stirred across her cheek, feather-light, as intimate as his thumb which remained on her lips. He was so close to her she could smell the scent of him, wild and clean as the forest, over the scent of the minerals in the mud that covered them.

She closed her eyes against the delicious agony of wanting a moment to last forever.

To escalate.

"I warned you there would be consequences if I took you prisoner," he said, the words playful, while his tone was anything but.

Was he going to kiss her? Even as a rational part of her knew they could never pull back from that again, a less rational part of her wanted the taste of his lips on hers, wanted to feel them.

She took her hand, as if it didn't matter it was mud-covered, and traced a possessive line down the hard plane of his jaw. She touched it to the fullness of his lip.

As if it didn't matter to him that it was mud-covered, he teased her finger gently, nibbled it with his teeth.

She felt the featherlight touch of his lip against the skin of her finger. Was it possible to die of sensation?

If this—the merest touch of his lips to something as inconsequential as her finger—could cause this unbelievable rise of sensation within her, what would it be like if he took her lips with his own?

She felt as if it would be a death of sorts.

The death of all she had been before, the rising up of something new, the rising up within her of a spirit that was stronger and more resilient than she had ever imagined, similar to that spirit that rose in her when she danced.

A place that was without thought, and without history.

Heaven.

Brazen with wanting, she slipped her muddy hands around the column of his neck, and pulled him down to her.

His weight settled on her more fully, chest to the soft curve of breast, hard stomach to delicate swell, muscled legs to slender ones, fused.

A whisper of sanity called her back from the brink.

And then called louder, *stop*.

It reminded her of the price of such a heated moment, lives changed forever.

But in that moment, she didn't care if there was a price.

And apparently neither did he.

Because his lips touched hers. The fact they were both mud-slicked only increased the danger, the sensuality, the delicious sense of being swept away, of not caring about what happened next, of being pulled by forces greater than themselves.

His very essence was in the way he kissed her.

Kiernan tasted, not of mud, but of rain in a storm, pure, clean, elemental. His kiss was tender, welcoming, and yet the strength and leashed passion were sizzling just below the surface.

It had been so long since Meredith had allowed anything or anyone to touch her, emotionally or physically.

She had not even known the hunger grew in her, waiting for something, someone to touch it off, to show her she was ravenous.

She was ravenous, and Kiernan was a feast of sensation.

Everything about him swirled around her—the light in his sapphire eyes, the line of his hard body against hers, the taste of his lips, the hollow of his mouth—all those broken places within her were being touched by sensation that was fulfilling and healing and exhilarating.

It was madness. Exquisite, delicious, compelling madness.

And she had to stop it. She had to.

Except that she was powerless, in the grip of something so amazing and wondrous she could not have stopped it if her very life depended on it. She was just not that strong.

But he was.

He pulled back from her, she saw strength and temptation war in his eyes, and she was astounded—and saddened—when his strength won. He pulled himself away from her, hesitated, dropped back down and placed one more tiny kiss on the corner of her lip, and then pulled his weight completely off her and stood gazing down at her.

Meredith saw control replace the heat in his eyes.

She watched awareness dawn in his eyes, saw his reluctant acquiescence to the guard he always surrounded himself with.

She knew, with a desperate sadness, this moment was over.

CHAPTER SIX

KIERNAN COMPOSED HIMSELF, held his hand to her. She took it, and her body made an unattractive slurping sound as he tugged, and then yanked hard to free her from the mud.

If he said he was sorry, she felt she would die.

But he did not say that, and she felt a strange sense of relief that she could tell he was not sorry. Not even a little bit.

And neither was she, even though the consequences of what had just happened hung over her.

Neither of them spoke, looking at each other, aware with an awareness that could not be denied once it had been acknowledged.

He dropped her hand, but not her gaze.

"Thank you," he said softly.

She knew exactly what he meant. That moment of being so alive, so incredibly vibrantly alive had been a gift to both of them.

She had not even been aware how much she lived in a state of numbness until she had experienced this wonderful hour with him. It had been carefree, and laughter-filled, wondrous. Meredith felt as if she had been exquisitely and fully alive in a way she had not been for a long, long time.

If she ever had been that alive, that fully engaged, that spontaneous, that filled with wonder for the simple, unexpected miracle of life.

Still, leaving the utter and absolute magic of the moment, Meredith felt as if she was going to cry.

She covered the intensity of the moment by pasting a smile on her face. "You're welcome. People pay big money for the mud treatment at the spa."

"Yes," he said, watching her closely, as if he knew she was covering, as if he knew exactly how fake that smile was. "I know."

And of course he would know. Because that was his world. Spas and yachts and polo ponies.

His world. He had playfully said he would take her prisoner, but the truth was his world was a prison in many ways.

And he could not invite her into it.

She did not have the pedigree of a woman he would ever be allowed to love.

Love. How had that word, absolutely taboo in her relationship with him, slipped past all her guards and come into her mind?

But now that it had come, Meredith was so aware how this moment was going to have a tremendous cost to her. Because, she had ever so briefly glimpsed his heart. Because she had seen the coolness leave his eyes and be replaced with tenderness. Yes, this moment had come at a tremendous price to her. Because she had let her guard down, too.

For a moment she had wanted things she could not have. Ached for them.

Still, if she had this choice to make over, how would she do it? Would she play it safe and stay in the ballroom, tolerating his wooden performance, allowing his mask to remain impenetrable?

No, she would change nothing. She would forever be grateful she had risked so much to let him out of his world, and his prison. Even if it had only been a brief reprieve.

And in return, hadn't she been let out of hers?

He turned from her, but not before she caught the deeply thoughtful look on his face, as if every realization she was having was also occurring to him.

He walked back through the fern barrier, leapt into the hot springs completely clothed. She watched his easy strength, as he did a powerful crawl that carried him across the pool to the cascading water of the falls. She quelled the primitive awareness that tried to rise in her.

Instead, she dove into the pool, too. Her skin had never felt so open to sensation. He had climbed up on a ledge underneath the falls, and she saw the remnants of their day falling off of him as if it had never happened.

It was time to clean herself of the residue of the day, too. She swam across the pool and pulled herself up on the ledge beside him.

The fresh, cold water was shocking on her heated skin. It pummeled her, was nearly punishing in its intensity.

Though she and Kiernan stood side by side, Meredith was painfully aware some distance now separated them, keeping their worlds separate even in the glorious intimacy of the cascading water world that they shared.

She slid him a look and felt her breath catch in her throat.

His face was raised to the water, his eyes closed as

what was left of the mud melted out of his hair and dissolved off his face, revealing each perfect feature: the cut of high cheekbones, the straight line of his nose, the faint cleft of his chin.

The white of Andy's shirt had reemerged, but the shirt had turned transparent under the water, and clung to the hard lines of Kiernan's chest. She could see the dark pebble of his nipple, the slight indent of each rib, the hollow of a taut, hard belly. It made her mouth go dry with a powerful sense of craving.

To touch. To taste. To have. To hold.

Impossible thoughts. Ones that would only bring more grief to her if she allowed them any power at all. Hadn't her life held quite enough grief?

Was it the coldness of the water after all that heat, or her awareness of him that was making her quiver?

Meredith felt herself wanting to save this moment, to remember the absolute beauty of it—and of him—forever.

He finally turned and dove cleanly off the ledge, cutting the water with his body. With that same swift, sure stroke, Kiernan made his way back across the mineral pond to where he had set the baskets. How long ago? An hour? A little longer than an hour?

How could so much change in such a short amount of time?

She dove in, too, emerged from the pond, dripping, and flinging back the wetness of her hair. She saw, from the brief heat in his eyes before he turned away, that Molly's shirt must have become as transparent as Andy's.

She glanced down. And she had accused him of boring underwear? Her bra—a utilitarian sports model made for athletic support while dancing—showed clearly through the wet fabric. But from the look on his face you would have thought she was wearing a bra made out of silk and lace!

She shoved by him, and rummaged through the baskets, tucked a towel quickly around herself and then silently handed him a towel and a change of clothing.

Was there the faintest smirk on his face from how quickly she had wrapped herself up?

"You're prepared," he said.

Yes. And no. There were some things you could not prepare for. Like the fact you hoped a man would tease you about being a prude, like the fact it was so hard to let go of a perfect day.

But he didn't tease her, or linger. He ducked behind a rock on one side of the glade and she on the other. She did not want to think of him naked in a garden, but she knew the temptation of Eve in that moment, and fought it with her small amount of remaining strength.

The trip back was eerily silent, as if they were both contemplating what had happened and how to go forward—or back—from that place.

Meredith drove back through the same service entrance to Chatam Palace. On the way in she had to stop and show ID, and her palace pass. She did not miss the stunned look on the face of the guard as he recognized the prince squished in the seat beside her. He practically tossed her ID back through her window, drew himself to attention and saluted rigidly.

It could not have been a better reminder of who the man beside her *really* was.

And the look of shock on the guard's face to see the prince in such a humble vehicle with a member of the palace staff, could not have been a better reminder of who she really was, too.

He was not Andy. She was not Molly.

He was a prince, born to position, power and prestige. She was a servant's daughter, a woman who had given birth to an illegitimate child, a person with so much history and so much baggage.

She let the prince out, barely looking at him. He barely looked at her.

They did not say goodbye.

Meredith wondered if he would show up for their scheduled dance session tomorrow.

Would she?

The whole thing had become fraught with a danger that she did not know how to handle.

And yet, even that tingling sensation of danger as she drove away from the palace after dropping Kiernan off there, served as a reminder.

She was alive.

She was alive, and for the first time in a long, long time, she was aware of being deeply grateful that she was alive. The pain. The glory. The potential to be hurt. The potential to love. It was all part of the most incredible dance.

There was that word again.

Love.

"Forbidden to me," Meredith said. Because of who he was. Because of who she was, and especially because of where she had already been in the name of love.

But of course, what had more power than forbidden fruit?

When Prince Kiernan walked through the doors of the ballroom the next morning, Meredith did not know whether she was relieved he had come, or sorry that she had to be tested some more.

He was right on time as always.

They exchanged perfunctory greetings. She put on the music. He took her hand, placed his other with care on her waist.

The trip to the hot springs had obviously been an error in every way it was possible for something to be an error.

This was turning out to be just like the day she had ridden his horse and they had danced in the courtyard to the chamber music spilling out the palace windows.

Prince Kiernan's guard came down, but only temporarily!

And when it went back up, it went way up!

After half an hour of tolerating a wooden performance from him, Meredith was not tingling with awareness of being alive at all! She was tingling with frustration. Was he dancing this badly just to put her off? Maybe he was hoping she would cancel the whole thing. And maybe she should.

Except she couldn't. It was too late now to start over with someone else. The girls, rehearsing separately, at her studio, had practiced to perfection. They were there night and day, putting heart and soul into this.

She wasn't letting them down because Prince Kiernan was the most confoundedly stubborn man in the world.

But really, enough was enough!

"This is excruciating," she said, pulling away from him, folding her arms across her chest and glaring at him.

Somewhere under that cool, composed mask was the man who had chased her, laughter-filled, through the mud.

"I warned you I had no talent."

"Call somebody," she snapped at him. "It's like a

game show where you have a lifeline. Call somebody, and use your princely powers. Have them find us the movie *Dancing with Heaven*. And deliver it. Right here. Right now."

It was an impossible request. The movie was old. It would probably be extremely difficult if not impossible to find.

For a moment he looked like he might argue, but then he chose not to, probably because he wanted to do just about anything rather than dance.

With her.

With some new tension in the air between them. Harnessed, it would make for an absolutely electrical dance performance.

Resisted, it would make for a disastrous dance performance.

He took a cell phone out of his pocket, and placed a call.

"Tell them not to forget the popcorn," she said darkly. "And I'd like something to drink, too."

"You're being very bossy," he said. "As usual."

Within minutes his cell phone rang back. "It's set up in the theater room," he said.

"Can't we watch it here?"

"No, we can't. I'm not sitting on an icy cold floor to watch a movie. Not even for you."

Not even for you. She heard something there that she knew instantly he had not intended for her to hear. Something that implied he would do anything for her, up to and including going to the ends of the earth.

She deliberately quelled the beating of her heart and followed the prince to where he held open the ballroom doors for her.

It was the first time Meredith had been in the private

areas of the interior of the palace. The ballroom, along with the throne room, and a gallery of collected art was in the public wing of the palace, open to anyone who went there on a tour day.

Now, Prince Kiernan led her through an arched door flanked by two palace guards who saluted him smartly. The door led into the private family quarters of the palace.

They were in a grand entranceway, a formal living room on one side, a curving staircase on the other. The richness of it was startling: original old masters paintings, Persian rugs, priceless antiques, draperies and furniture upholstered in heavy brocaded silks. A chandelier that put the ones in the ballroom to shame spattered light over the staircase and entry.

Kiernan noticed none of it as he marched her up the wide stairs, under the portraits of his ancestors, many of whom looked just like him, and all of whom looked disapproving.

"What a happy looking lot," she muttered. "They have aloofness down to a fine art."

He glanced at the portraits. "Don't they?" With *approval*.

So *that's* where he got his rigidity!

"Maybe I'm wasting my time trying to break past something that has been bred into each Chatam for hundreds of years." And that they were proud of to *boot*.

"I've been trying to tell you."

And maybe if she hadn't been stupid enough to take him on that excursion yesterday, she would have believed him.

"This floor is where guests stay," he said, exiting the staircase that still spiraled magnificently upward. He led her down a wide corridor.

Bedroom doors were open along either side of the hallway and she peeked in without trying to appear too interested. The bedrooms, six in all, three on either side of the hallway were done in muted, tasteful colors. The décor had the flavor and feel of pictures Meredith had seen of very upscale boutique hotels.

It occurred to Meredith that princes and presidents, prime ministers, princesses and prima donnas had all walked down these corridors.

It reminded her who the man beside her *really* was, and she felt a whisper of awe. He opened the door to a room at the end of the long hallway.

Meredith tried not to gape. The "theater room" was really the most posh of private theaters. The walls were padded white leather panels with soft, muted light pouring out from behind them. The carpets were rich, dark gold with a raised crown pattern in yet darker gold. There were three tiers of theater style chairs in soft, buttery distressed leather. Each chair had a light underneath it that subtly illuminated the aisle. The chairs faced a screen as large as any Meredith had ever seen.

Two chairs were in front of all the others, and Kiernan gestured to one of them. Obviously she was sitting in a chair that would normally be slated for the most important of VIP's. She settled into the chair.

"Who's the last person who sat here?" She could not stop herself from asking.

If Kiernan thought the question odd he was polite enough not to let on. "I think it was the president of the United States. Nice man."

Never had she been more aware of who Kiernan really was.

And who she really was.

A man in a white jacket, very much like the one she

had borrowed from Andy, arrived with a steaming hot bowl of popcorn for each of them. He pushed a button on the side of her seat, and a tray emerged from the armrest.

"I was kidding about the popcorn," she hissed at Kiernan, but she took the bowl anyway.

"A drink, miss?"

Part of her was so intimidated by her surroundings, she wanted to just say no, to be that invisible girl who had accompanied her mother to work on occasion.

But another part of her thought she might never have on opportunity like this again, so, she was making the most of it. She decided to see how flummoxed the man would be if she ordered something completely exotic and off the wall—especially for ten o'clock in the morning. "Oh, sure. I'll have a virgin chi-chi."

The servant didn't even blink, just took the prince's order and glided away only to return a few minutes later.

"My apologies," he said quietly. "We didn't have the fresh coconut milk today."

She had to stifle a giggle. A desire to tease and say, *see that that doesn't happen again.* Instead, she met the man's eyes, and saw the warmth in them, and the lack of judgment.

"Can I get you anything else?"

"No, thank you for your kindness," she said. And she meant it.

She took a sip, and sighed. The drink, even without the fresh coconut milk was absolute ambrosia.

The movie came on. For the first few minutes Meredith was so self-conscious that Prince Kiernan was beside her. It felt as if she was on a first date, and they were afraid to hold hands.

Dancing with Heaven was dated and hokey, but the dance sequences were incredible, sizzling with tension and sensuality.

Though she had seen this movie a dozen times, Meredith was soon lost in the story of a spoiled self-centered young woman who walked by a dance studio called Heaven, peeked in the window, and was entranced by what she saw there. The dance instructor was a bitter older man whose career had been lost to an injury. He taught dance only for the money, because he had to.

Through what Meredith considered some the best dance sequences ever written, the young woman moved beyond her superficial and cynical attitude toward life and the instructor came to have hope again.

Wildly romantic, and sizzling with the sexual chemistry between the two, the instructor fought taking advantage of the young heiress's growing love for him, but in the end he succumbed to the love he had for her and the unlikely couple, united through dance, lived happily ever after.

What had made her insist the prince see this ridiculous and unrealistic piece of fluff?

When it was over, Meredith was aware of tears sliding down her face. She wiped at them quickly before the lights came up, set down her empty glass and her equally empty popcorn dish.

"Now you know what I expect of you. I'll see myself out. See you in the morning."

Kiernan saw that Meredith was not meeting his eyes. Something about the movie had upset her.

He ordered himself to let it go, especially after yesterday. Not that he wanted to think about yesterday.

He'd kissed her, and it hadn't been a little buss on

the cheek, either. No, it had been the kind of kiss that blew something wide open in a man, the kind of kiss that a man did not stop thinking about once it had happened.

It was the kind of kiss that made a man evaluate his own life and find it seemed empty, and without color.

The problem was they had been pretending to be ordinary.

And between an ordinary man and an ordinary woman maybe such things could happen without consequences.

But in his world? If he went where that kiss invited him to go, *begged* him to go, the world she knew would be over.

She had trusted him with her deepest secrets. How would she like those secrets to be exposed to the world? If he let his guard down again, if he allowed things to develop between them, Meredith would find her past at the center ring of a three-ring circus. Pictures of her baby would be dug up. Her mother's past would be investigated. Her ex would be found and asked for comments on her character.

So, even though the movie had upset her, it would be best to let her go.

And yet he couldn't.

He stepped in front of her.

"Are you upset?" he asked quietly.

She looked panicked. "No. I just need to go. I need to—"

"You're upset," he said. "Why? Did the movie upset you?"

"No, I—"

"Please don't lie to me," he said. "You've never done it before, and you have no talent for it."

She was silent.

He tipped her chin. "Did it remind you of your baby's father?" he asked softly. "Is that the way you felt about him?"

He remembered the sizzling sensuality between the on-screen couple, and he felt a little pang of, good grief, *envy*. But this wasn't about him. He could actually feel her trembling, trying to hold herself together.

"Talk to me, Meredith."

"It had a happy ending," she whispered. "I deplore happy endings! If it weren't for the dance sequences, I would have never asked you to watch such drivel!"

But he was stuck at the *I deplore happy endings* part. How could anyone so young and so vibrant have stopped believing in a happy ending for herself?

"My baby's father was older than me, twenty-two. He was new to the neighborhood, and all the girls were swooning over his curly hair and his suave way. I was thrilled that he singled me out for his attention. Thrilled."

Kiernan felt something like rage building in him at the man he had never met, the man who had used her so terribly, manipulated and fooled a young girl. But he said nothing, fearing that if he spoke, she would clam up.

And he sensed she needed to talk, she needed to say these things she had been holding inside. And he needed to be man enough to listen, without being distracted by her lips and the memory of their taste, without wanting *more* for himself. Without putting his needs ahead of her own.

"If I had married Michael, my baby's father, it would have been a disaster," she said. "I can see that now. As hard as it was for me and my mom to make ends meet, it would have only been harder with him. You want to know how bad my taste is in men? Do you want to know?"

He saw the regret in her eyes and the pain, and he wanted to know everything about her. Everything.

"He didn't even come to the funeral."

She began to sob.

And he did what he should have done yesterday in the car, what he had wanted to do.

He pulled her into his chest, and ran his hand up and down her back, soothing her, encouraging her. *Let it out.*

"I loved him, madly. I guess maybe I held on to this fantasy he was going to come to his senses, do the right thing, come back and rescue me. Prove to my mother she was wrong. Love us."

If he could have, he would have banished the shame from her face.

"Kiernan," she said softly, "he didn't care one fig about me. Not one. And I fooled myself into thinking he did. How can a person ever trust themselves after something like that? How?"

He loved that she had called him his name, no formal address. Wasn't that what was happening between them? And what he was fighting against?

Deepening trust. Friendship. Boundaries blurring. But as he let her cry against him, he knew it was more. Mere friendship was not something that would put his guard up so high. And mere friendship would never have him feeling a nameless fury at the man who had cruelly used her, walked away from his responsibilities, broken her heart as if it was nothing.

His fury at a man he had never met abated as he

became aware of Meredith pressed against him, felt the sacredness of her trust, and this moment.

He was not sure that he had ever felt as much a man as he did right now.

"You deserved so much better," he finally said.

"Did I?" She sounded skeptical.

He put her away from him, looked deep into the lovely green of her eyes. "Yes," he said furiously, "you did. As for trusting yourself? My God, cut yourself some slack. You were a child. Sixteen. Is that what you said?"

"Seventeen when Carly was born."

"A child," he repeated firmly. "Taken advantage of by an adult man. His behavior was despicable. To be honest? I'd like to track him down and give him a good thrashing!"

She actually giggled a little at that. "Maybe the dungeon?"

He felt relieved that she was coming around, that he saw a spark of light in her eyes. "Exactly! Extra rats!"

"Thank you," she said, quietly.

"I'm not finished. As for not trusting yourself? Meredith, you have taken these life experiences and made it your mission to change things for others. Do you remember what I said to you when you thanked me for not allowing you to fall off the horse?"

"Yes," she whispered, "You said it's not how you fall that matters. You said everyone falls. You said it was how you got up that counted."

He was intensely flattered that she had heard him so completely. He spoke quietly and firmly. "And how you are getting up counts, Meredith. Helping those Wentworth girls honors your baby. And your mother. And you."

She gave him a watery smile, pulled away from him,

not quite convinced. "Oh, God, look at me. A blithering idiot. In front of a prince, no less."

And she turned, he could tell she was going to flee, and so he caught her arm. "I'm not letting you go, not just yet. Let's have tea first."

Just in case he was beginning to think he was irresistible, she said, "Will it have the little cream puff swans?"

"Yes," he said. "It will."

He guided her out of the theater and to the elevator at the end of the hallway and took her to his private apartment.

"It's beautiful," she said, standing in the doorway, as if afraid to come in. And maybe he should have thought this out better.

Once she had been in here, would he ever be completely free of her? Or would he see her walking around, pausing in front of each painting like this, always?

"Is it you who loves Monet?" she asked.

He nodded.

"Me, too. I have several reproductions of his work."

"I understand," Kiernan said, "that he was near-sighted. That wonderful dreamy, hazy quality in his landscapes was not artistic license but how he actually saw the world. You know what I like about that?"

She looked at him.

"His handicap was his greatest gift. Your hardships, Meredith?"

She was looking at him as if he had a lifeline to throw her. And he hoped he did.

"Your hardships are what make you what you are. Amazingly strong, and yet good. Your goodness shines out of you like a light."

He turned away to look after tea. But not before he

saw that maybe he had said exactly the right thing after all, but maybe not enough of it. She did not look entirely convinced.

He had tea set up on the balcony that overlooked the palace grounds and the stunning views of Chatam.

"Instead of allowing your falls to break you," he insisted quietly, sitting her down, "you have found your strength."

"No, really I haven't."

Now he felt honor-bound not to let her go until she was convinced. Of her own goodness. Of her innate strength. Of the fact that she had to let go of all that shame. Of the fact she was earning her way, by the way she chose to live her life, to a new future.

"I want to know every single thing there is to know about you. I want to know how you've become the remarkable woman you are today." And he meant that.

She looked wildly toward the exit, but then she met his eyes. But just to keep him from feeling too powerful, then she looked at the tray of goodies a servant was bringing in.

"Oh," she said. "The cream puffs."

"I know how to get your secrets out of you, Meredith."

"There's nothing remarkable about me."

"Ah, well, let me decide."

She mulled that over, and then sighed. Almost surrender. He passed her the tray. She took a cream puff, and sighed again. When she bit into it and closed her eyes he knew her surrender was complete.

They talked for a long, long time. It was deep and it was true and it was real. He felt as if they could sit there and talk forever.

It was late in the afternoon before Meredith looked at her watch, gasped, and made her excuses. Within seconds she was gone. Kiernan was not sure he had ever felt he had connected with someone so deeply, had ever inspired trust such as he had just experienced from her.

Kiernan sat for a long time in a suite that felt suddenly cold and empty for all the priceless art and furniture that surrounded him. It felt as if the life had gone out of it when Meredith had.

Without her the room just seemed stuffy. And stodgy.

He'd liked having her here in his very private space. He'd liked watching the movie with her and how she had not tried to hide the fact she was awed that a president had sat in her chair. He liked how she had acknowledged Bernard who had brought their popcorn and drinks, not treated him as if he was invisible, the way Tiffany always had.

And damn it, he'd liked that movie.

Silly piece of fluff that it was, it was somehow about people finding the courage to be what they were meant to be, to bring themselves to the world, to overcome the strictures of their assigned roles and embrace what was real for them.

And, finally, he had loved how she had come into his space, and how between cream puffs and his genuine interest and concern for her she had become so open. And liked what the afternoon told him about her.

Above all things, Meredith was courageous.

A hardscrabble upbringing, too many losses for one so young, and yet he saw no self-pity in her. She was taking the challenges life had given her and turning them into her greatest assets. She had a quiet bravery to get on with her life.

That's what she was asking of him. To bring his

courage to the dance floor. To dance without barriers, without a mask, and without a safety net.

She was asking him to be who he had been, ever so briefly, when they had chased each other through the mud.

Wholly alive. Completely, unselfconsciously himself.

No guards. No barriers.

And she was asking him to be who he had been just now: deep and compassionate.

Really, what she was asking of him would require more courage than just about anything he had ever done. At the hot springs he had shown that unguarded self to her. And again today there had been something so open and unprotected about their interaction after the movie.

Prince Kiernan felt as if he stood on the very edge of a cliff. Did he take a leap of faith, trusting if he jumped something—or someone—would catch him? Or did he turn away?

"For her sake," he said to himself, "You turn away."

But he didn't know if he was powerful enough to do that. He knew he wanted these last days with her before it was over.

So he could have moments and memories, a secret, something sacredly private in his life, to savor when she was gone.

CHAPTER SEVEN

"FROM THE TOP," Meredith said. Today's dancing session, she knew, was going no better than yesterday's. The movie had changed nothing.

No, that was not true.

It had changed everything.

It had changed her. Maybe not the movie, exactly, but what had happened after.

When Kiernan had held her in her arms, it had felt as if everything she had been fighting for since the death of her mother and baby—independence, strength, self-reliance—it had felt as if those things were melting.

As if some terrible truth had unfolded.

All those qualities that she had striven toward were just distractions from the real truth. And the truth was she was so terribly alone in this world.

And for a moment, for an exquisite, tender moment in the arms of her country's most powerful man, she had not felt that. Sitting beside him on the balcony of his exquisite apartment, surveying all his kingdom, pouring out her heart, telling her secrets, she had not felt that.

For the first time in forever, Meredith had not felt alone.

And it was the most addictive sensation she had ever

felt. She wanted to feel it again. She wanted to never let go of it.

Worse, she had a tormented sense that, though Kiernan walked with kings and presidents, she had seen what was most *real* about him. It was the laughter at the hot springs, it was his confidence in his horse, it was the tenderness in his eyes as he had listened to her yesterday.

And she had to guard against the feeling that he caused in her.

Because just like the wealthy heiress and the dance instructor in the movie, their worlds were so far apart. But unlike the movie, which was pure escapist fantasy after all, they could never be joined. And the sooner she accepted the absoluteness of that the better.

This morning she felt only embarrassed that she had revealed herself so totally to him. Talked, not just about Michael and Carly, which was bad enough, but about her childhood, growing up with a single mom in Wentworth, and then repeating her family's history by becoming one herself.

She'd told him about ballet, and her mother's hope and losing the scholarship when she became pregnant. She'd told him about those desperate days after Carly was born, her mother being there for her, despite her disappointments, Millie loving the baby, but never quite forgiving her daughter.

She told him about the insurance settlement after the tragedy that allowed her to own her own dance studio and form No Princes, and how guilty she felt that her dreams were coming true because the people she had loved the most had died.

Oh, yes, she had said way, way too much. And today, it was affecting *her* dancing.

She was the one with the guard up. She was the one who could not open herself completely. She was the one who could not be vulnerable on the dance floor. She was trying desperately to take back the ground she had lost yesterday.

And she was failing him. Because she could not let him in anymore. She could not be open.

She was as rigid and closed as the prince had been on that first day. It was the worst of ironies that now he seemed as open as she was closed!

"What's wrong?" he asked.

The tender concern in his eyes was what was wrong! The fact she was foolishly, unrealistically falling in love with him was what was wrong!

"You know what?" he said, snapping his fingers. "I know I have the power to fix whatever is wrong!"

Yes, he did. He could get down on one knee and say that though the time had been short he realized he was crazy about her. That he couldn't live without her.

All this work. All this time with No Princes and Meredith's weaknesses were unabated! She despised that about herself.

"One call," he said, and smiled at her and left the room.

When he returned he had a paper bag with him, and with the flourish of a magician about to produce a rabbit, he opened it and handed her a crumpled white piece of fabric.

"Ta-da," he said as she shook out the white smock.

"What is this?"

"I think I've figured it out," he said, pulling another smock from the bag and tugging it over his own shirt.

It had Andy embossed across the breast.

She stared down at the smock in her hand. Sure enough, he had unearthed Molly's smock.

"Remember when you told me this kind of dancing is like acting?"

Meredith nodded.

"Well, I'm going to be Andy for the rest of the rehearsals. And you're going to be Molly."

She stared at him stunned. She wanted to refuse. She wanted to get out of this with her heart in one piece.

But she could not resist the temptation of the absolute brilliance of it. If she could pretend to be someone else, if she could pretend he was someone else, there was a slim chance she could save this thing from catastrophe. And maybe, at the same time, she could save herself from the catastrophe of an unattainable love.

But it seemed the responsibility for saving things had been wrested from her. Kiernan took charge. He went and put on the music, turned and gazed at her, then held out his hands to her.

"Shall we dance, Molly?"

She could only nod. She went and took his hands, felt the way they fit together. Her resolve, which she could have sworn was made of stone, melted at his touch.

"Remember Andy?" he said, smiling down at her as they began the opening waltz.

She gave herself over to this chance to save the dance. "Isn't he that devilish boy who won't do his homework?"

"Except he did watch *Dancing with Heaven*."

"Used class time, though."

"That's true."

Kiernan had those opening steps down *perfect*. A little awkwardness, a faint stiffness, a resolve to keep his distance in his posture.

The transition was coming.

"Andy," she reminded him, getting into the spirit of this, embracing it, "winks at the teacher and makes her blush."

And Kiernan became that young fellow—on the verge of manhood, able to tie his teacher in knots with a blink of sapphire-colored eyes.

"I think he makes her drop things, too," Meredith conceded, and her blush was real. "And forget what she's teaching at all."

Kiernan smiled at her with Andy's wicked devil-may-care-delight. Through dance he became the young man who rode motorcycles, and wore black leather. He was the guy who drove too fast and broke rules.

Something about playing the role of the bad boy unleashed Kiernan. He was playful. He was commanding. He was mischievous. He was *bad*.

His hips moved!

They moved to the next transition, and Kiernan released her hand. He claimed the dance floor as his own.

He claimed it. Then he owned it.

Meredith's mouth dropped open as he tore off the smock that said Andy on it, and tossed it to the floor.

Before her eyes, Kiernan became the man who liked loud music and smoky bars, and girls in too-short skirts and low-cut tops who wiggle their hips when they dance. He became the guy who cooled off in the town fountain, claimed Landers Rock as his own, kept his hat on during the anthem.

He became a man so comfortable with himself that he would delight in swimming in the sea naked under the moonlight.

And then came the final transition.

And he was no longer an immature young man, chasing skirts and adrenaline rushes, breaking rules just for the thrill of having said he had done it.

Now he was a man, claiming the woman he wanted to spend the rest of his life with.

He crossed the floor to her, and they went seamlessly to the finale—dancing together as if nothing else in the world existed except each other, and the heat, the chemistry between them.

Meredith was not Meredith. She was Molly.

And something about being Molly unleashed her just as much as being Andy had unleashed him. She didn't have a history. She was just a girl from the kitchen who wanted something more out of life: not drudgery, but a hint of excitement wherever she could find it.

By playing Molly, Meredith came to understand her younger self.

And forgive her.

Finally, with both of them breathless, the music stopped. But Kiernan did not let her go. He stared at her silently, his eyes saying what his mouth did not.

She pulled away from him. Her smile was tremulous.

"It was perfect," she breathed.

"I know. I could feel it."

She had to get hold of herself; despite this breakthrough she had to find the line between professional and personal. She had to get over the feeling of wanting to take his lips and taste them, of wanting more than she could have, of wanting more than he could offer her.

"You know what would be brilliant?" Meredith said crisply. "We can alter the real performance dream sequence slightly so that it is Andy and Molly, and Andy transforms into a prince."

He was looking at her just as he had on the balcony of his private suite. With eyes that saw right through her professional blither-blather to the longing that was underneath.

She was only human.

And he was only human.

If she was going to keep this thing on the tracks until the performance at *An Evening to Remember* she had to make a drastic decision, and she had to make it right now.

"You know what this means, don't you?"

He shook his head.

"We're finished."

"Finished?"

"We're done, Prince Kiernan." It was self-preservation. She could not dance like that with him every day until the performance and keep her heart on ice, keep him from seeing what was blossoming inside her.

Like a flower that would be cut.

"We've got two practices left," he said, frowning at her.

"No," she said firmly, with false brightness, "there's nothing left to practice. Nothing. I don't think we should do it again. I don't want to lose the freshness of what we just did. We're done, Prince Kiernan. The next time we do that dance, it will be at *An Evening to Remember.*"

Instead of looking relieved that dance class was finally over, Kiernan looked stunned.

She felt stunned, too. She was ending it. The suddenness of it made her head spin. And she felt bereft. It was over. They would have one final dance together, but it was already over. She was ending this craziness right here and right now.

"So," she said with forced cheer, holding out her

hand to shake his, "good work, Your Highness. I'll see you opening night of Blossom Week, for *An Evening to Remember*. Gosh. Only a few nights away. How did that happen?"

But instead of shaking her hand, two business people who had done good work together, the prince took her hand, held it, looked with deep and stripping thoughtfulness into her eyes. Then he bowed over her hand, and placed his lips to it.

Meredith could feel that familiar devastating quiver begin in her toes.

"No," he said, straightening and gazing at her.

"No? No *what*?"

"No, it won't be opening night before we meet again."

"It won't?" It felt just like their first meeting, when he had told her she couldn't be Meredith Whitmore. He said things with the certainty of one who had the power to change reality, who *always* had his own way.

"You've shown me your world, Meredith," Kiernan said quietly. "You gave that to me freely, expecting nothing in return. You gave me a gift. But I would like to give you something in return, a gift of my own. Come experience an evening in my world."

Her mouth opened to say *no*. It wasn't possible. She was trying to protect herself. He was storming the walls.

"It's the least I can do for you. I'll send a car to pick you up tonight. We'll have a farewell dinner on the yacht."

Farewell. Did his voice have an odd catch in it when he said that?

Say *no*. Every single thing in her that wanted to survive screamed at her to say no.

But what woman, no matter how strong, no matter how independent, no matter how much or how desperately she wanted to protect her own heart could say no to an evening with a prince, a date out of a dream?

It wasn't as if she could get her hopes up. He'd been very clear. A farewell dinner. One last time to be alone together. The next time they saw each other would be very public, for their performance.

On pure impulse, Meredith decided she would give herself this. She would not or could not walk away from the incredible gift he was offering her.

She would take it, greedily. One night. One last thing to remember him by, to hold to her when these days of dancing with him, laughing with him, baring her soul to him, were but a distant memory.

"Yes," she whispered. "That would be lovely."

It wasn't a *date*, Meredith told herself as she obsessed about what to wear and how to do her hair and her makeup and her nails. It wasn't a date. He had not called it that. A gift, he had said, and even though she knew she should have tried harder to resist the temptation, now that she hadn't, she was giving herself over to the gift wholeheartedly.

She intended to not think about a future that did not include him. She was just going to take it moment by moment, and enjoy it without contemplating what that enjoyment might cost her later.

Hadn't she done that before? Exchanged heated looks and stolen kisses with no thought of the consequences?

No, it was different this time. She was a different person than she had been back then. Wasn't she?

And so, trying to keep her doubts on the back burner, with her makeup subtle and perfect, her nails varnished with clear lacquer, dressed in a simple black cocktail dress with a matching shawl, her hair upswept, the most expensive jewelry she could afford—tiny diamonds set in white gold—twinkling at her ears, she went down her stairs, escorted by a uniformed driver, to where the limousine awaited her. She thanked God that all the years of dancing made her able to handle the incredibly high heels—and the pre-performance jitters—with seeming aplomb.

Passersby and neighbors had stopped to gawk at the black limo, and the chauffeur holding it open for her.

It was not one of the official palace vehicles with the House of Chatam emblem on the door, but still she waved like a celebrity walking the red carpet, and slid inside the door.

The luxury of it was absolutely sumptuous. She was offered a glass of champagne, which she refused. The windows of the backseat were darkly tinted, so all the people staring at her as they passed could not see her staring back at them.

The car glided through the streets of Chatam into the harbor area, and finally arrived at a private dock. The yacht, called *Royal Blue*, bobbed gently on its moorings.

A carpet had been laid out to prevent her high heels from slipping through the wide-spaced wooden planks of the dock. Light spilled out every window of the yacht, danced down the dock and splashed out over inky dark waters.

The lights illuminated interior rooms. It wasn't a boat. It was a floating palace.

And against the midnight darkness of the sky, she could see Prince Kiernan. He was outside on an upper deck, silhouetted by the lights behind him, leaning on a railing, waiting.

For her.

She wanted to run to him, as if he was not a prince at all, but her safe place in this unfamiliar world of incredible wealth.

Instead, she walked up the carpet, and up the slightly swaying gangway with all the pose and grace years of dancing had given her. She knew his eyes were only for her, and she breathed it in, intending to enjoy every second of this gift.

The crew saluted her, and her prince waited at the top of the gangway.

Prince Kieran greeted her by meeting her eyes and holding her gaze for a long time, until her heart was beating crazily in her throat. Then he took her hand, much as he had in the ballroom, bowed low over it, and kissed it.

"Welcome," he said, and his eyes swept her.

Every moment she had taken with her hair and her makeup, her jewelry and her dress was rewarded with the light in his eyes. Except that he seemed to be memorizing her. He had said *welcome*, but really, hadn't he meant goodbye?

"You are so beautiful," he said, the faintest hoarseness in that cultured voice.

"Thank you," she stammered. She could have told him he looked beautiful, too, because he did, dressed in a dark suit with a crisp white shirt under it. At the moment, Kiernan was every girl's fairy-tale prince.

"Come," he said, and he slipped his hand in hers, and led her to a deeply padded white leather bench in the bow of the boat.

As the crew called muted orders to each other the

yacht floated out of its slip and they headed out of the mouth of the harbor.

"I just have to let you know in advance, that as hard as I tried to completely clear my calendar for this evening, I'm expecting an overseas call from the Minister of Business. I'll have to take it. I hope it will be brief, but possibly not. I hope you won't be bored."

Meredith was used to these kinds of interruptions from their dance classes.

"Bored? How could I be bored when I have this to experience?" She gestured over the view of dark sea, the island growing more distant. "It looks like a place out of a dream."

The lights of Chatam, reflected in the dark water, grew further away.

"It will be breezy now that we're underway. Do you want to go in?"

She shook her head, and he opened a storage unit under a leather bench, found a light blanket and settled it on her shoulders. Then Kiernan pressed against her to lend her his warmth.

As the boat cut quietly around the crags of the island, she found she and Kiernan talked easily of small things. The girls' excitement for the upcoming performance, Erin Fisher's remarkable talent and potential, Prince Adrian's recovery from his injury, the overseas call Kiernan was expecting about a business deal that could mean good things for the future of Chatam.

After half an hour of following the rugged coastline of Chatam, the yacht pulled into a small cove, the engines were cut, and the quiet encircled them as she heard the chain for the anchor drop.

"It's called Firefly Cove," he said. "Can you see why?"

"Oh," she breathed as thousands and thousands of small lights pricked the darkness, "it is so beautiful."

The breeze picked up, and he took the blanket and offered her his hand. They went inside.

It was as beautiful as outside.

There was really nothing to indicate they were on a boat, except for the huge windows and the slight bobbing motion.

Other than that the décor was fabulous—modern furniture covered in rich linens, paintings, rugs, an incredible chandelier hung over a dining table set for two with the most exquisite china.

All of it could have made her feel totally out of place and uncomfortable. But Kiernan was with her, teasing, laughing, putting her at ease.

Dinner came out, course after course of the most incredible food, priceless wines that an ordinary girl like her would never have tasted under other circumstances.

But rather than being intimidated Meredith delighted in the new experiences, made easy because of how her prince guided her through them.

They went back out on the deck for after-dinner coffee, he draped the blanket around her shoulders again, and tucked her into him. They sat amongst the fireflies and talked. At first of light things: the exquisiteness of the food they had just eaten, the rareness of the wines, the extraordinary beauty of the fireflies; the stars that filled the night sky.

But Meredith found herself yearning for his trust, the same trust that she had shown him the day they had watched the movie.

With a certain boldness, she took his hand, and said, "Tell me how you came to earn all those horrible nicknames. Playboy Prince. Prince of Heartaches. Prince Heartbreaker. I feel as if I've come to know you, and those names seem untrue and unfair."

But was it? Wasn't he setting her up for heartbreak right now? Without even knowing it? He'd been clear. Tonight was not hello. It was goodbye.

But she wasn't allowing herself to think of that.

No, she was staying in this moment: the gentle sway of the sea beneath her, his hand in hers, his shoulder touching hers.

She was staying in this moment, and moving it toward deeper intimacy even if that was crazy. She wanted him to know, even after they'd said goodbye, that she had known his heart.

"Thank you," he said with such sincerity, as if she had *seen* him that she quivered from it, and could not resist moving a little more closely into his warmth. "Though, of those titles, the Playboy Prince was probably neither untrue nor unfair."

He recounted his eighteenth summer. "I found myself free, in between getting out of private school and going into the military. Until I was eighteen, my mother had been very vigilant in restricting the press's access to me. And women hadn't been part of my all-male world, except as something desired from a distance, movie star posters on dorm room walls. So, I wasn't quite used to the onslaught of interest on both fronts.

"And like many young men of that age, I embraced all the perks of that freedom and none of the responsibility. Unfortunately, my forum was so public. There was a frenzy, like a new rock star had been unveiled to the world. I didn't see a dark side or a downside. I was flattered by the attention of the press and the young women. I dated every beautiful woman who showed the least interest in me."

"And that was many," Meredith said dryly.

Still, she could feel the openness of him, and something sighed within her. She had trusted him, and now he was trusting her.

"That's what I mean about the Playboy Prince title having truth to it," he said ruefully. "But after that summer of my whole life becoming so public, I became more discerning, and certainly more cynical. I started to understand that very few of those young women were really interested in *me*. It was all about the title, the lifestyle, and the fairy tale. I could be with the most beautiful woman in the world and feel so abjectly lonely.

"But for a short while, I searched, almost frantically for *the* one. I'm sure I broke hearts right and left because I could tell after the first or second date that it just wasn't going to work, and I extricated myself quickly. Somehow, though, I was always the one seen as responsible for the fact others pinned their unrealistic hopes and dreams on me."

Was that what she was doing? By sitting here, enjoying his world and his company, was she investing, again, in unrealistic hopes and dreams?

Just one night. She would give herself that. It wasn't really pinning hopes and dreams on him. It was about knowing him as completely as she could before she let him go back to his world, and she went back to hers.

"I'd known Francine Lacourte since I was a child," Kiernan continued. "We'd always been close, always the best of friends."

"The duchess." She felt the faintest pang of jealousy at the way he said that name. With a tender reverence.

"She was the funniest, smartest woman I ever met.

She was also the deepest. She had a quality about her, a glow that was so attractive. She shunned publicity, which I loved."

"You were engaged to her, weren't you?"

"Ever so briefly."

"And you broke it off, bringing us to nickname number two, the Prince of Heartaches. Because she never recovered, did she?"

Which, now that she thought about it, Meredith could see was a very real danger.

But Kiernan smiled absently. "The truth that no one knows? I didn't break it off. She did."

He was telling her a truth that no one else knew? That amount of trust felt exquisite.

"But that's not what the press said! In fact, they still say she is in mourning for you. She has become very reclusive. I don't think I've seen one photograph of her in the paper since you broke with her. And that's years ago. It really is like she has disappeared off the face of the earth."

"Our friends at the press take a fact—like Francine being reclusive—and then they build a story around it that suits their purposes. It has nothing to do with the truth. For a while there was even a rumor started by one of the most bottom feeding of all the publications that I had murdered her. How ridiculous is that?"

"That's terrible!"

"I am going to tell you a truth that very few people on this earth know. I know I don't have to tell you how deeply private this conversation is."

Again, Meredith relished this trust he had in her, even as she acknowledged it moved her dangerously closer to pinning unrealistic hopes and dreams on him!

"That depth and quality and glow in Francine that I

found so attractive? She had a deep spiritual longing. Francine joined a convent. She had wanted to do so for a long, long time. She loved me, I think. But not the way she loved God."

"She's a nun?" Meredith breathed, thinking of pictures of her that had been republished after his broken engagement to Tiffany Wells. Francine Lacourte was gorgeous, the last person one would think of as a nun!

He nodded. "She chose a cloister. Can you imagine the nightmare her new life would have been if the paparazzi got hold of that? Because I have a network around me that can protect me from the worst of their viciousness, I chose to let them create the story that titillated the world."

"You protected her," Meredith whispered.

"I don't really see it like that. She gave me incredible gifts in the times we spent together. I was able to return to her the privacy she so treasured."

"By taking the heat."

"Well, as I say, I have a well-oiled machine around me that protects me from the worst of it. The press can say whatever they want. I'm quite adept at dodging the arrows, not letting them affect me at all. So, if I could do that for Francine, why wouldn't I?"

Hadn't she known this for weeks? In her heart, with her sense of *knowing* him growing? That the prince was actually the opposite of how he was portrayed by the press?

"And then you graduated to being the Prince Heartbreaker," Meredith said.

"Tiffany came along later, and I was well aware it was *time*. Very subtle pressure was being brought on me to find a suitable partner. I had been deeply hurt by Francine's choice, even as I commended her for making it. At some level I think I was looking for a woman who was the antithesis of her, which Tiffany certainly was. Bubbly. Beautiful. Light. Lively. Tiffany Wells was certain of her womanly wiles in this seductive, confident way that initially I was bowled over by."

There were few men who wouldn't be, Meredith thought, with just a touch of envy.

"I was a mature man. She was a mature woman. Eventually, we did what mature adults do," he admitted. "I'm ashamed to say for the longest time I mistook the sexual sizzle between us as love. Still, we were extremely responsible. Double protected.

"But as that sexual sizzle had cooled to an occasional hiss, I realized it was really the only thing we had in common."

"She bored you!" Meredith deduced.

He looked pained. "Her constant chatter about *nothing* made my head hurt. I was feeling increasingly disillusioned and she, unfortunately, seemed increasingly enamored.

"I told her it was over. She told me she was pregnant."

Meredith gasped, but he held her hand tighter, looked at her deeply. "No, Meredith, it is not your story. I did not abandon a pregnant woman."

CHAPTER EIGHT

PRINCE KIERNAN TOLD Meredith the rest of the story haltingly. After overcoming the initial shock of Tiffany's announcement he had weighed his options with the sense of urgency that the situation demanded.

He had done what he felt was the honorable thing, a man prepared to accept full responsibility for his moment of indiscretion.

His engagement had been announced, and they had set a date for the very near future, so that Tiffany's pregnancy would not be showing at the wedding. The press had gone into a feeding frenzy. Tiffany had appeared to adore the attention as much as he was appalled by it. She was "caught" out shopping for her gown and flowers, having bachelorette celebrations with her friends, even looking at bassinettes.

"When we were together, we could not have one moment of privacy. The cameras were always there, we were chased, questions were shouted, the press always seemed to know where we were. Now, uncharitably, I wonder if she didn't tip them off. But regardless, our lives became helicopters flying over the palace, the yacht, the polo fields, men with cameras up trees and in shrubs.

"On this point, Meredith, you were absolutely correct

in what you said to me on the day we began dance practice. Romance is glorious entertainment. It sells newspapers and magazines and it ups ratings. Interest in us, as a couple, was nothing short of insatiable."

"How horrible!" Meredith said.

"You'd think," he said dryly. "Tiffany loved every moment of it. For me, it felt as if I was riding a runaway train that I couldn't stop and couldn't get off of."

"But you did stop it. But what of the baby? In all the publicity that followed, I never once heard she was pregnant."

"Because she wasn't."

"What?"

"Before that incident it had never occurred to me that a person—particularly one who claimed to love you—could be capable of a deception of such monstrous proportions as that. Luckily for me, the truth was revealed before we were married. Unluckily, it was the night before the wedding."

He went on to say a loyal servant, assigned to Tiffany, had come in obvious distress late on the eve of the wedding to tell him something that under normal circumstances he would have found embarrassing. But the fact that *pregnant* Tiffany was having her period had saved him. Despite the lateness of the hour, he had confronted Tiffany immediately, and the wedding had been cancelled.

But now the whole world saw him as the man who had coldheartedly broken a bride's heart on the eve of all her dreams coming true. The press seemed tickled by the new role they had assigned him, Prince Heartbreaker.

Tiffany, on the other hand, seemed to be enjoying the attention as much as ever, photographed often, sunglasses in place, shoulders slumped, enthusiastically playing the part of the party who was suffering the most and who had been grievously wronged.

"Why on earth wouldn't you let the world know what and who she really is?" Meredith demanded, shocked at how protective she felt of him. "Why are you taking the brunt of the whole world's disappointment that the fairy tale has fallen apart?"

"Now you sound like Adrian." He paused before he spoke. "I saw something in Tiffany's desperate attempt to capture me that was not evil. It was very sad and very sick. I glimpsed a frightening fragility behind her mask of supreme confidence.

"How fragile only a very few people know. Tiffany had attempted suicide after I uncovered her deception."

"It sounds like more manipulation to me," Meredith said angrily.

"Regardless, I was not blameless. I gave in to temptation, let go of control when I most needed to keep it. I put Tiffany in a position where she hoped for more than what I was prepared to offer, I put myself in a position of extreme vulnerability.

"I don't think Tiffany could have handled her deception being made public, the scorn that would have been heaped on her."

"She certainly seems to handle it being heaped on you rather well. Her total lack of culpability enrages me, Kiernan."

He shrugged. "I've been putting up with the attacks of the press since I was a young man. I'm basically indifferent to what they have to say."

"You protected her, too. Even though she is not the least deserving of your protection!"

He shrugged it off. "Don't read too much into it, Meredith. I'm no hero."

"Just a prince," she said and was rewarded with his laughter.

"Just a man," he said. "Underneath it all, just a man."

But a good one, she thought. A man with a sense of decency and honor. A man who had not abandoned the woman he thought carried his child.

The man of her dreams. So, so easy to fall in love with him.

A steward came and whispered in his ear.

"I'm so sorry. That's the call I have to take."

The truth? She was glad for a moment alone to sort through the new surge of emotion she felt at his innate decency, at his deeply ingrained sense of honor.

"Don't think anything of it," she assured him. She didn't mind. She wanted to sit here and savor his trust and the world he had opened to her. But she badly needed distance, too.

The steward brought her a refill for her coffee, the day's paper, and a selection of magazines.

After staring pensively at the sea for a long time, she needed any kind of distraction to stop the whirling of her thoughts. She picked up the paper.

In the entertainment section she stopped dead.

There was a picture of society beauty Brianna Morrison under the headline Prince Heartbreaker's New Victim?

But Miss Morrison looked like anything but a victim! She was hugging a gossamer green dress to her, her choice for the Blossom Week Ball, the event that would culminate the week's celebrations.

"I couldn't believe it when I was asked," she gushed to the interviewer. "It is like a dream come true."

It seemed something went very still in Meredith. She was sharing the prince's yacht tonight. But he had been very clear. This was farewell.

The prince giving the peasant girl a final gift of himself before moving back to his real life.

But he had asked another woman to the ball.

Well, of course he had. Meredith had always known she didn't belong in this world. Brianna Morrison's family was old money, the Morrisons owned factories and businesses, real estate, and shipping yards.

And tonight he had said pressure, subtle or not, was being brought on him to find a suitable partner. Brianna was beautiful and accomplished. Her family's interests and the interests of the Chatams had been linked for centuries.

And then there was Meredith Whitmore. A dance instructor, more devoted to her charity than her business, a woman with a hard past.

No, the prince had decided to give his dance instructor a lovely night out.

A small token of appreciation. He had never claimed it was anything more than a way of saying goodbye to her and the world they had shared for a few light-filled days.

She had been crazy to encourage his confidences, some part of her hoping and praying she was in some way suitable for his world and that he would see it.

She set down the paper and called the steward. "Could we go back to Chatam, please? I'm not feeling well."

In seconds, Kiernan was at her side.

"I hope you didn't end your phone call on my behalf," she said coolly, not wanting to see the concern on his face, deliberately looking to the sea that was beginning to chop under a strengthening wind.

"Of course I did! You're not feeling well? It's probably the roughening sea, but I can have my physician waiting at the dock."

"No, it's not that serious," she said, trying not to melt at his tender concern, trying to steel herself against it. "I'm sure it is the sea. I just need to go home."

"I'll give the order to get underway immediately." He rose, scanned her face, and frowned.

Then he saw the open newspaper.

She leaned forward to close it, but he stayed her hand, bent over and scanned the headline.

"You read this?" he asked her.

She said nothing, tilted her chin proudly, refused to look at him.

"Is this why you're suddenly not feeling well? It was arranged months ago," he said quietly.

"It's none of my business. I'm well aware I don't belong in your world, Prince Kiernan. That this has been a nice little treat for a peasant you've taken a liking to."

"It is not that I don't think you belong in my world," he said with a touch of heat. "That's not it at all! And I don't think of you as a peasant."

"Of course not," she said woodenly.

"Meredith, you don't understand the repercussions of being seen publicly with me."

"I might use the wrong fork?"

"Stop it."

"I thought this was such a nice outfit. You probably noticed it was off the rack."

"I noticed no such thing. It's a gorgeous outfit. You are gorgeous."

"Apparently. Gorgeous enough to see you privately."

"Meredith, you need to understand the moment you are seen with me, publicly, your life will never be the same again. Taking you to that ball would be like throwing you into a pail of piranhas. The press would have started to rip you apart. You've told me some shattering secrets about yourself. Do you want those secrets on all the front pages providing titillation for the mob? I won't do that to you."

"Of course," she said, "You're protecting me. That's what you do."

"I am trying to protect you," he said. "A little appreciation might be in order."

"Appreciation? You deluded fool."

He looked stunned by that and that made her happy in an angry sort of way so she kept going.

"You've chosen women in the past that build you up with their weakness, who need their big strong prince to protect them, but I'm not like that."

"I've chosen weak women?" he sputtered.

"It's obvious."

"I'm sorry I ever told you a personal thing about myself."

She was sorry he had, too. Because it had made her hope for things she couldn't have. She couldn't stop herself now if she wanted to.

"I'm a girl from Wentworth. Do you think there's anything in your world that could frighten me? I've walked in places where I've had a knife hidden under my coat. I've been hungry, for God's sake. And so exhausted from working and raising a baby I couldn't even hold my feet under me. I've buried my child. And my mother. Do you think anything in your cozy, pampered little world could frighten me? The press? I could handle the press with both my hands tied behind my back.

"Don't you dare pretend that's about protecting me. Your Royal Highness, you are protecting yourself. You don't want anyone to know about tonight. Or about me. I'm the sullied girl from the wrong side of the tracks. You're right. They would dig up my whole sordid past. What an embarrassment to you! To be romantically linked to the likes of me!"

"I told you everything there is to know about me," he said quietly, "and you would reach that conclusion?"

"That's right!" she snapped, her anger making her feel so much more powerful than her despair. "It's all about you!"

She banished everything in her that was weak. There would be plenty of time for crying when she got home.

After the trust they had shared, the intimacy of their dinner, the growing friendship of the last few days, this was *exactly* what was needed.

Distance.

Anger.

Distrust.

And finally, when she got home, then there would be time for the despair that could only be brought on from believing, even briefly, in unrealistic dreams.

But when she got home, she realized she had done it on purpose, created that terrible scene on purpose, driven a wedge between them on purpose.

Because she had done the dumbest thing of her whole life, even dumber than believing Michael Morgan was a prince.

She had come to love a real prince. And she did not think she could survive another love going wrong.

And the truth? How could it possibly go right?

"What is wrong with you?" Adrian asked Kiernan the next day.

"What do you mean by that?"

"Kiernan! You're not yourself. You're impatient. You're snapping at people. You're canceling engagements."

"What engagement?"

"You were supposed to bring Brianna Morrison to the ball. The worst thing you could have done is cancelled that. One more tearstained face attached to your name. She's been getting ready for months. Prince Heartbreaker rides again."

"Is that a direct quote from the tabs?"

"No. That is so much kinder than the tabs. They're having a heyday at your expense. This morning they showed Brianna Morrison throwing her ball dress off a bridge into Chatam River."

"Make sure she's charged with littering a public waterway."

"Kiernan! That's cold! You are just about the most hated man on the planet right now."

Yes. And by the only one that mattered, too.

Adrian was watching him closely. "And there's that look again."

"What look?"

"I don't know. Moody. *Desperate.*"

"Adrian, just leave it alone," he said wearily.

"If something is wrong, I want to help."

"You can't. Not unless you can learn to dance in—" he glanced at his watch "—about four hours."

Adrian's eyes widened. "I should have known."

"What?" Kiernan said. What had he inadvertently revealed?

"Dragon-heart. She's at the bottom of this."

Kiernan stepped in very close to his young cousin. "Don't you ever call her that again within my hearing. Do you understand me?"

"She did something to make you so mad," Adrian said. "I know it."

"No, she didn't," Kiernan said. "I did. I did something that made me so mad. I gave my trust to the wrong person."

Adrian was watching him, his brow drawn down in puzzlement. "I'll be damned," he said. "You aren't angry. You're in love."

Kiernan thought it would be an excellent time for a vehement denial. But when he opened his mouth, the denial didn't come out.

"With Dra— Meredith?"

"It doesn't matter. It's going nowhere. After I revealed my deepest truths to her do you know what she did? She called me a deluded fool!"

Adrian actually smiled.

"It's not funny."

"No, it's a cause for celebration. Finally, someone who will take you to task when you need it."

"Don't side with her. You don't even like her."

"Actually, I always did like her. Immensely. She wouldn't settle for anything less than my best. She was strong and sure of herself and intimidating as hell, but I liked her a great deal."

"Do you know what she said to me? She said I deliberately chose weak women. What do you think about that?"

"That she's unusually astute. Finally, someone who will tell you exactly what they think instead of filtering it through what they think you want to hear."

"You never told me you thought my women were weak," Kiernan said accusingly.

"Because they were heart-stoppingly beautiful. I thought that probably made up for it. I always knew you never dated anyone who would require you to be more than you were before. I thought it was your choice. That you had decided love would take a minor role in your life. Behind your duties."

"I think I had thought that. Until I fell in love. It doesn't accept minor roles."

"So, you do love her!" Adrian crowed.

"It doesn't matter. I had her to the yacht for dinner last night, and she opened the paper and saw I was escorting Brianna to the ball. She left in a temper."

"Uh, real world to Kiernan: any woman who is having dinner with a man will be upset to find he has plans with another woman for later in the week."

"I told her it had been planned for months."

"Instead of *I'll cancel immediately*?" Adrian shook his head and tut-tutted.

"I told her it was for her own good. She has some things in her past I don't want the press to get their hands on. I was protecting her!"

"I bet she loved that one."

"It's true!"

"She isn't the kind who would take kindly to you micromanaging her world."

"She's not. She doesn't trust me. I showed her everything I was, and she rejected it. She believed the worst of me, just like everyone else is so quick to do."

"Kiernan, you are making excuses."

"Why would I do that?"

"You are terrified of what that woman would require of you."

"I'm not."

"Don't you get it? This is your chance. You might only get one. Take it. Be happy. Do something for yourself for once. Go sweep old Dragon-heart right off her feet."

"Don't call her that."

"I can't believe I missed it!" His cousin became uncharacteristically serious. "She's worthy of you, Kiernan. She's strong. And spunky. She's probably the best thing that ever happened to you. Don't let it slip away."

And suddenly Kiernan thought of how awful she had looked when she had left the yacht. She was afraid. He'd taken that personally, as if it was about him. But of course she was afraid! She had lost everything to love once before. She was terrified to believe in him, to trust.

And Adrian was right. He was *not* doing the right thing. Sulking because she didn't trust him, not seeing what lay beneath that lack of trust. Why should she trust the world? Or him? Had the world brought her good things? No, it had taken them. Had love brought her good things? No, it had shattered her.

Instead of seeing that, he had insisted on making it about him.

He was going to have to be a better man than that to be worthy of her. He was going to have to go get her from that lonely world she had fled to in her fear and distrust.

Kiernan of Chatam was going to have to learn what it really meant to be a woman's prince.

Something sighed within him.

He was ready for the challenge. He was about to go rescue the maiden from the dragon of fear and loneliness she had allowed to take up residence in her heart.

"I don't know what to do," he admitted.

Adrian smiled. "Sure, you do. You have to woo the girl. Just the same as any old Joe out there on the street. She isn't going to just fall at your feet because you're a prince, you know. For God's sake, she runs an organization called No Princes. Playing hard to get is going to be a point of pride with her.

"And don't look so solemn. For once in your life, Kiernan, have some fun."

The show must go on, Meredith thought as she found herself, in a white smock in a crowded dressing room, waiting, her heart nearly pounding out of her chest. She had never been this nervous about a performance.

"Miss Whit," one of the girls said excitedly. "He's here. He's come. Ohmygod, he's the most glorious man I ever laid me eyes on."

"*My* eyes," Meredith corrected woodenly.

"The music's starting," Erin whispered. "Oh, I can't believe this is happening to me. My production is becoming a reality. I just looked out the curtain. Miss Whit, it's standing room only out there."

For them. She had to pull this off for them, her girls, all that she had left in her world.

"I'm on," Erin said. "I'm so scared."

Meredith shook herself out of her own fear, and went and gave her protégée a hard hug.

"Dazzle them!" she said firmly.

And then she stood in the wings. And despite her gloom, her heart began to swell with pride as she saw Erin's vision come to life. The girls in the opening number carried the buckets of cleaning ladies, or wore waitresses' uniforms. Some of them carried school bags. All had on too much makeup. They were hanging around a street lamp, targets for trouble.

And here came trouble. Boys in carpenter's aprons, and baker's hats, leather jackets with cigarettes dangling from their lips.

The girls and the guys were dancing together, shy, flirtatious, bold, by turns.

And then Erin, who had been given the starring role, was front and center in her white smock that said Molly over the pocket, and she was staring worshipfully at a boy in a white jacket that said Andy on the pocket.

The lights went off them, and the empty spot on the stage filled with mist.

It was time for the dream sequence.

The three-step bridal waltz began to play, and feeling as if she was made of wood, Meredith came on stage.

Kiernan was coming toward her.

How unfair that while she suffered, he looked better than ever! No doubt to make his costume more realistic, he had a few days growth of unshaven beard.

Meredith went to him, felt her hand settle into his, his hand on her waist.

Her eyes closed against the pain of it.

Last time.

Even as she thought it, she could hear a whisper ripple through the crowd. It became a rumble as the spotlight fell on them, and recognition of Kiernan grew.

"You look awful," he said in her ear.

"I've been working very hard with the girls," she whispered back haughtily. She stumbled slightly. He covered for her.

"Liar. Pining for me."

She tried to hide her shock. "Why would a girl like me pine for you?" she snapped at him. "We both know it's impossible."

He was looking at her way too hard.

"You're afraid," he said in an undertone. "It was never really horses you were afraid of. It was this."

The crowd was going crazy. Not only had they recognized their prince, but he was doing something completely unexpected. Kiernan and Meredith picked up the pace, and he found his feet. She tried not to look at the expression on his face.

"Don't be silly," she told him in an undertone. "I told you nothing about your world frightens me."

"You're afraid of loving me. You have been from the moment we met."

"Arrogant ass," she hissed.

"Stubborn lass," he shot back.

She could feel the fire between them coming out in the way they were dancing. It was unrehearsed, but the audience was reacting to the pure sizzling chemistry.

She couldn't look away from him. His look had become so fierce. So tender. So protective. So filled with longing.

He knew the truth, anyway, why try to hide it? Why not let it come out in this dance?

It occurred to her that even if he couldn't have her, even if she would never be suitable for his world, that he wanted her, and that he wished things were not the way they were.

One last time, she would give herself this gift.

She would be Molly and he would be Andy, just two crazy ordinary kids in love. Everything changed the moment she made that decision. She would say to him with this dance what she intended to never admit to him in person.

She found her feet. She found his rhythm.

And they danced. She let go of all her armor. She let go of all her past hurt. She let go of all her fear. She let go of that little worm of self-doubt that she was not good enough.

Meredith danced as she had never danced, every single secret thing she had ever felt right out there in the open for all the world to see.

At some point, she was not Molly. Not at all. She was completely herself, Meredith Whitmore.

For this one priceless moment, she didn't care who saw her truth. Though thousands watched, they were alone, dancing for each other.

And then he let her go, and the crowd became frenzied as he moved into his solo piece.

He tore off the white smock.

And suddenly she saw his truth. It was not dancing as Andy that allowed him to dance like this.

It was dancing as Kiernan.

Everything he truly was came out now: sensual, strong, commanding, tender. Everything.

By the time he came across the floor to her that one last time, the tears were streaming down her face for the gift he had given her.

He had given her his everything.

He had put every single thing he was into that dance. Not for the audience who was going wild with delight.

Not for the girls who cheered and screamed from the wings.

For her. He stared down at her.

It was not in any way a scripted part of the performance. He took her lips with exquisite tenderness.

She tasted him, savored, tried to memorize it.

With the cheering in the building so loud it sounded as if the rafters would collapse on them, she pulled away from the heaven of his lips, touched his cheek. Though the whole world watched it felt, still, as if they were alone.

Goodbye.

"Thank you," she whispered through her tears. "Thank you, Kiernan." And then she turned and fled.

CHAPTER NINE

It was the day after *An Evening to Remember.*
Meredith's phone had been ringing off the hook, but
she wouldn't answer.

Still, people left messages. They wanted lessons from
her dance school. They wanted to donate money to No
Princes.

Erin Fisher's excited voice told her she had been offered a full scholarship to Chatam University.

The press wanted to know what it felt like to dance
with a prince. They wanted to know if she had been the
one to teach the prince with two left feet to dance like
that. They especially wanted to know if there was *something* going on, or if it had all been a performance.

After several hours of the phone ringing she went
and pulled the connection out of the wall.

She didn't want to talk to anybody.

Maybe not for a long, long time.

Just as she had suspected, the video had been posted
online within seconds of the performance finishing.

The website had collapsed this morning, for the first
time in its history, from too many hits on that video.

"Most of those hits from me," Meredith admitted
ruefully. She had watched their dance together at least
a dozen times before the site had crashed.

Seeing something in it, basking in it.

Was love too strong a word?

Probably. She used it anyway.

There was a knock on her door. She hoped the press had not discovered where she lived. She tried to ignore it, but it came again, more insistent than the last time. She pulled a pillow over her head. More rapping.

"Meredith, open the damn door before I kick it down!"

She pulled the pillow away from her face, sat up, stunned, hugging it to her.

"I mean it. I'm counting to three."

She went and peered out her security peephole.

"One."

Prince Kiernan of Chatam was out on her stoop, in an Andy jacket and dark glasses.

"Two."

She threw open the door, and then didn't know what to do. Throw herself at him? Play it cool? Weep? Laugh?

"Lo, Molly," he said casually.

Don't melt.

"Just wondered if you might like to come down to the pub with me. We'll have a pint and throw some darts."

"Once you lose the sunglasses everyone will know who you are." Plus, they'd probably all seen the Andy getup on the video. He'd be swamped.

"Let's live dangerously. I'll leave the glasses on. You can tell people I have a black eye from fighting for your honor."

"Kiernan—"

"Andy," he told her sternly.

"Okay, Andy." She folded her arms protectively over her chest. "Why are you doing this?"

He hesitated a heartbeat, lifted the glasses so she could look into his eyes. "I want us to get to know each other. Like this. As Andy and Molly. Without the pressure of the press following us and speculating. I want us to build a solid foundation before I introduce you to the world. I want you to know I have your back when they start coming at you."

"You're going to introduce me to the world?" she whispered. "You're going to have my back?"

"Meredith, I miss you. Not seeing you was like living in a world without the sun. It was dark and it was cold."

She could feel the utter truth of it to her toenails.

"I miss the freedom I felt with you," he went on quietly. "I miss the sense of being myself in a way I never was before. I miss being spontaneous. I miss having fun. Will you come out and play with me? Please?"

She nodded, not trusting herself to speak.

"Come on, then. Your chariot awaits."

She could not resist him. She had never been able to resist him.

"I'm in my pajamas."

"So you are. Ghastly things, too. I picture you in white lace."

She gulped from the heat in his eyes.

"Go change," he said, and there was no missing the fact she had just been issued a royal order.

"Royal pain in the butt," she muttered, but she stood back from the door, and let him in.

Surely once he saw how ordinary people lived—tiny quarters, hotplate, faded furniture—he would realize he was in the wrong world and turn tail and run.

But he didn't. True to Andy he went and flung himself on her worse-for-wear couch, picked up a book she hadn't looked at for weeks and raised wicked eyebrows at her.

"Did you dream of me when you read this?" he asked.

"No!" She went and slammed her bedroom door, made herself put on the outfit—faded jeans, a prim blouse—that was the least like the one she had worn the other night on the yacht. It was the casual outfit of an ordinary girl.

But when she reemerged from the bedroom, the look in his eyes made her feel like a queen.

Feeling as if she was in a dream, Meredith followed him down the steep stairs that led from her apartment to the alley. Leaning at the bottom of the stairs was the most horrible-looking bike she had ever seen.

Kiernan straddled it, lowered his sunglasses, patted the handlebars. "Get on."

"Are you kidding? You'll kill us both."

"Ah, but what a way to go."

"There is that," she said, with a sigh. She settled herself on the handlebars.

His bike riding was terrible. She suspected he could barely ride a bike solo, let alone riding double. He got off to a shaky start, nearly crashing three times before they got out of her laneway.

Once he got into the main street he was even more hazardous, weaving in and out of traffic, wobbling in front of a double-decker bus.

"Give 'em the bird, love," he called when someone honked angrily when he wobbled out in front of them.

She giggled and did just that.

At the pub, true to his word, he left the glasses on.

She thought people might recognize him, but perhaps because of the plain lucridness of the whole thought that a prince would be in the neighborhood pub, no one did.

They ordered fish and chips, had a pint of tap beer, they threw darts. Then they got back on the bike and he took the long way home, pedaling along the river. She wasn't sure if her heart was beating that fast because of all the times he nearly dumped them both in the inky water of the Chatam Channel, or because she was so exhilarated by this experience.

"Where is this going?" Meredith asked sternly when he dropped her at her doorstep with a light kiss on the nose.

"My whole life," he said solemnly, "I've known where everything was going. I've always had an agenda, a pro-tocol, a map, a plan. The very first time I saw you dance, I knew you had something I needed.

"I didn't know what it was, but whatever it was, it was what made me say yes to learning the number for *An Evening to Remember*."

"And do you know what it was now?" she asked, curious, intrigued despite herself.

"Passion," he said. "My whole life has been about order and control. And when I saw you dance that day I caught a glimpse of what I had missed. The thing is, I felt bereft that I had missed it.

"Meredith, you take me to places I have never been before. And I don't mean a hot spring or a pub. Places inside myself that I have never been before. Now that I've been there, I can't live with the thought of not going there anymore."

He kissed her on the nose again. "I'll see you to-morrow."

"Look," she said, trying to gain some control back, "I just can't put my whole life on hold because you want me to take you places!"

He laughed, and leaned close to her. "But I've been saving my money so I can get us a Triple Widgie Hot Fudge Sundae from Lawrence's. To share."

"That's incredibly hard to resist," she admitted.

"The sundae or me?"

"The sharing."

"Ah." He looked at her long and hard. "Embrace it, Molly. Just embrace it."

"All right." She surrendered.

And that's what she did. She put her whole life on hold.

But not really.

She just embraced a different life.

Carefree and full of adventure.

Over the next few weeks, as Andy and Molly, they biked every inch of that island. They discovered hidden beaches. They ate ice cream at roadside stands. They laughed until their sides hurt. They went to movies. They roller-skated.

And just when she was getting used to it all, that familiar knock came on the door, but it was not Andy who stood there. Not this time.

This time it was Prince Kiernan of Chatam, in dark suit trousers and a jacket, a crisp white shirt, a dark silk tie.

He bowed low over her hand, kissed it.

"Aren't we going bike riding?" she asked.

"I love your world, Meredith, but now it's time for you to come into mine."

"I—I— I'll have to change," she said, casting a

disparaging look down at her faded T-shirt, her pedal pushers, and old sneakers.

"Only your clothes," he said quietly. "Nothing else. Don't change one other thing about you. Promise me."

"I promise," she said, and scooted back into her bedroom to find something suitable to wear for an outing with a prince. A few minutes later, in a pencil skirt of white linen and a blue silk top, she joined him.

"Are you ready for this?" he asked, holding out his hand to her.

"Ready for what, exactly?" She took his hand, gazed up at him, still unable to quite grasp that a prince was wooing an ordinary girl like her.

"My mother wants to meet you."

"She does?" Meredith gulped. "Why?"

"Because I told her I've met the woman I intend to spend the rest of my life with."

Meredith took a step back from him, not sure she had heard him correctly, her heart beating an ecstatic tattoo within her chest. "But you haven't told me that yet!"

He cocked his head at her, and grinned. "I guess I just did."

She flew into his arms, and it felt like going home. It felt exactly the way she had wanted to feel her whole life.

"You know how I feel right now?" she whispered into his chest. "I feel safe. And protected. I feel cared about. I feel cherished."

"You make me feel those things, too," he whispered back.

"And I feel absolutely terrified. Your mother? That makes everything seem rather official."

"You see, that's the thing. After you've met my

mother, it's going to be official. You're going to be my girl. And then my fiancée. And then my wife."

"Huh. Is that your excuse for a proposal?"

He laughed. "No. Just forewarning you of what's to come." And then he frowned. "If you can handle the pressure. You won't believe the pressure, Meredith. I'm afraid your life will never be the same. Be sure you know what you want before you walk out that door with me."

But she had been sure a long time ago. She knew exactly what she wanted. She placed her hand back in his, and felt her whole world was complete.

Someone with a camera had already discovered the limousine parked at her curb, because this time the royal emblem shone gold on the door. The camera was raised and their picture was taken getting into the car together.

He sighed.

But she squeezed his hand and laughed.

"I may be terrified of your mother," she said, as he settled in the deep leather of the seat beside her, "but I'm not afraid of anything else about being with you. Nothing." She laid her head on his shoulder and soaked in the strength and solidity of him, soaked in how very right it felt to be at his side.

For a moment there was the most comfortable of silences between them.

"Did you hear that?" he asked, as the car pulled away.

"I'm sorry, did I hear what?"

He looked out the window, twisted over his shoulder to look behind them, settled back with a puzzled look on his face.

"Meredith, I could have sworn I heard a baby laugh."

She smiled, and the feeling of everything in the world being absolutely right deepened around her.

"No," she said softly, "I didn't hear it. But I felt it. I felt it all the way to my soul."

Kiernan raised his hand to knock on the door of his mother's quarters. He'd been annoyed that upon delivering Meredith his mother had dismissed him with an instruction to come back in an hour. She had drawn Meredith in and closed the door firmly behind them.

He knew his mother! The inquisition had probably started. Especially after Tiffany, whom his mother had not liked from the beginning, Queen Aleda would feel justified in asking aggressive questions, making quick judgments. Meredith was probably backed into a corner, quivering and in tears.

But as he stood at the door, he was astounded to hear laughter coming through the closed door. He knocked and opened it.

Both women looked up. Meredith was seated, his mother looking over her shoulder. He saw he had underestimated Meredith again. He was going to have to stop doing that.

He noticed his mother had one hand resting companionably on Meredith's shoulder. His mother did not touch people!

Both women were focused on something on the table, and he recognized what it was.

"Photo albums?" he sputtered. "You've just met!"

"Never too soon to look at pictures of you as a baby," Meredith said. "That one of you in the tub? Adorable."

"The tub picture?" He glared at his mother, outraged.

"What could I do?" Queen Aleda said with a smile. "Meredith asked me what my greatest treasure was."

And then the two women exchanged a glance, and he was silent, in awe of the fact their mutual love of him could make such a strong and instant bond between these two amazing women.

In the days and weeks that followed, Kiernan's amazement at Meredith grew and grew and grew.

The day after their first official public outing, when he had taken her to watch a royal horse run in the Chatam Cup, speculation began to run high. Some version of the picture of Meredith leaning over the royal box to kiss the nose of the horse had made every front page of every major paper around the world.

His press corps was instantly swamped with enquiries. When had he begun dating his dance instructor? Who was she? And especially, what was her background?

"This is the beginning," he'd told her. "How do you want to handle it?" Meredith called her own press conference.

Yes, she was dating the prince. Yes, they had met while she taught him the dance number for *An Evening to Remember*. No, she was not worried about his history, because she had a history of her own.

And in a strong, steady voice, without any apology Meredith had laid herself bare. All of it. Wentworth. The too-young pregnancy. Her abandonment by the father of her child. The baby. The lost dance dreams. The grinding poverty. The tragedy that took her mother and her child. The insurance money that had allowed her to start No Princes.

She had left the press without a single thing to dig

for. And instead of devouring her, the press had *adored* her honesty, and the fact she was just one of the people. Unlike so many celebrities that the press waited breathlessly to turn on, their love affair with Meredith was like his own.

And like that of all the people of Chatam.

The more they knew her, the more they loved her.

And she loved them right back. She became the star of every event they attended, the new and quickly beloved celebrity. From film festivals at Cannes to her first ski trip to catch the last spring snow in Colorado, she bewitched everyone who met her.

She was astonishingly at home, no matter where he took her.

But the part he loved the most was that none of it went to her head. She was still the girl he had first met. Maybe even more that girl as she came into herself, as love gave her a confidence and a glow that never turned off.

Meredith could be on the red carpet at a film premiere one day, and the next day she was just as at home on her bicycle, visiting a Chatam farmer's market. She delighted in surprising brides and grooms in Chatam on their wedding days by dropping by the reception to offer her good wishes.

When he begged her to allow him to offer her security, she just laughed at him. "I've already been through the worst life can give out, Kiernan. I'm not afraid."

And she really wasn't. Meredith was born to love. It seemed her capacity to give and receive love was endless.

And since he was the major benefactor of all that love, who was he to stop her?

Besides, he knew something he had not known a few

months ago, and probably would not have believed if someone had tried to tell him.

There were angels. And Meredith had two who protected and guided her. What other explanation for the series of coincidences that had brought them together? How had she landed right on his doorstep? How had Adrian come to be injured so that the right prince could meet her? How was it that Kiernan had gone against his own nature, and agreed to learn to dance? How was it he had seen something in her from the very beginning, that he could not resist?

From that first moment, watching her dance, Kiernan had known she held a secret that could change his life. Known it with his heart and not his head.

And only angels could have made him listen to his heart instead of his head.

But angels aside, there was no ignoring the very human side of what was happening to them.

He *wanted* her. He wanted her in every way that a man could want a woman. Their kisses were becoming more fevered. The times when they were alone were becoming a kind of torture of *wanting*.

The thing was, he would never take her without honor.

Never. What that other man had done to her was unconscionable. He would never be like him, never, ever remind Meredith of him. He would not use her obvious passion for him, or her willingness to have his way with her. He always backed away at the last possible moment.

There were honorable steps a man had to take to be with his woman. He had to earn his way there. It did not matter that it was his intention to marry her, and it was, even though he knew they had only known each other a short while, only months.

But he knew his own heart, too.

And he knew it was time.

CHAPTER TEN

MEREDITH WOKE UP to a sound at her window. Something was hitting against it. She groaned and pulled the pillow over her head.

Kiernan was probably right. She was going to have to move to a building with security. That was probably some fledging reporter out there hoping to get the shot that would make his career.

Despite her attempts to ignore it, the sound came again, louder. A scattering of pebbles across her pane.

And then louder yet!

She got up, annoyed. They were going to break the window! But when she shoved it up, and leaned out, ready to give someone a piece of her mind, it was Kiernan who stood below her.

"What are you doing?" Her annoyance now was completely faked. Sometimes she could still not believe this man, a prince outside, and a prince inside, too, was looking at her like that. With such open adoration in his eyes.

Of course the feeling was completely mutual!

"I have a surprise for you."

"What time is it?" she asked with completely faked grumpiness.

"Going on midnight."

"Kiernan, go home and go to bed."

"Quit pretending you can resist me. Get dressed and come down here."

She stuck out her tongue at him and slammed the window shut, but she quickly changed out of her pajamas, yanking on an old dance sweatsuit.

"I see you are working hard at impressing me," he said, kissing her on the nose as she reached the bottom of her stairs.

"As you are me," she teased back. "Waking me at midnight. I have work tomorrow. We don't all have lives of leisure."

This was said completely jokingly. She seemed, more than anyone else, to respect how hard he worked, and how many different directions he was pulled in a day. He was still savoring the newness of having someone at his side who was willing to back him up, to do whatever she needed to do to ease his burdens, to make his life simpler.

He held open the door of an unmarked car for her. Tonight as no other he did not want the press trailing them.

She snuggled under his arm. "What are you up to?"

But he wouldn't tell her.

They sailed through the roadblock he'd had put up to close the popular road, just for this one night. Meredith peeked out the car window with curiosity, and then recognition. "Are we going where I think we are going?"

The car stopped at the pull-out for Chatam Hot Springs. He held out his hand to her and drew her out of the car, led her up the path, lit by torches tonight, that led the way to the springs.

When they got there, he savored the look on her face. No detail had been overlooked.

There were torches flaming around the pool, but the bubbling waters of the springs were mostly illuminated by thousands upon thousands of candles that glowed from every rock and every surface.

"I didn't bring a suit," she whispered, looking around with that look he had come to live for.

A kind of *pinch me I must be dreaming* look.

"There's a change tent for you over there," he said. "You'll find a number of bathing suits to choose from."

She emerged from the tent a few minutes later, and he, already changed, was waiting on the edge of a rock with his feet dangling in the water. He smiled at her choice. Though there was staff here, they were invisible at the moment.

"The black one," he said with a shake of his head. "I was hoping for something skimpier. The red one, with the polka dots."

"How did you know about the red one with the polka dots?" she demanded.

"Because I picked each one myself, Meredith."

"That must have been very embarrassing for you," she said. "Careful, the press will dub you the pervert prince."

He leered at her playfully. "And let's hope it's deserved."

This is how it was with them. Endlessly playful. Teasing. Comfortable. Fun. And yet the respect between them also grew.

As did the heat.

As she crossed the slippery rock to him he could easily see that the black tank-style suit was so much more sexy than the polka dot bikini! Instead of sitting demurely beside him, Meredith pretended to touch his shoulders lovingly and then shoved with all her might.

And then turned and ran.

He caught up with her at the mud pool.

And they played in the mud, and swam and played some more until they were both exhausted with joy.

And then he sent her back to the change tent.

Where he knew all the rejected bathing suits had been whisked away, and in their place were designer gowns like the ones she had refused to let him buy for her for all the public outings they had attended.

While she changed, a table was set up for them and waiters appeared, along with a chef fussing about the primitive conditions he'd had to prepare his food in.

When she'd emerged from the change tent this time, Kiernan's mouth fell open. Meredith had stunned him with her beauty even in the off-the-rack dresses she insisted on wearing.

But now she had chosen the most racy of the gowns that he had picked out for her. It was red and low-cut.

She had even put on some of the jewelry he had put out for her, and a diamond necklace blazed at her neck and diamond droplets fell from her ears.

"I am looking at a princess," he said, bowing low over her hand and kissing it.

"I've told you *no* to this extravagance, Kiernan."

And yet, despite her protest, he could not help but notice that she was glowing with a certain feminine delight. She knew she looked incredible.

He led her to the table, laid out with fine linen and the best of china, and the waiters served a sumptuous feast.

She knew most of the palace staff by name, and addressed each of them.

When they had finished eating, she smiled at him. "Okay. I give it to you, you can't ever top this."

"But I will."

"You can't."

He called one of the waiters and a cooler was brought to their table. Inside it was one Triple Widgie Hot Fudge Sundae and two spoons.

In that perfect environment, their worlds combined effortlessly.

"I love it all," she said. "But you shouldn't have bought all the dresses, Kiernan. I can't accept them, and you probably can't return them."

"I'm afraid as my wife you'll be expected to keep a certain standard," he said. "And as your husband I will be proud to provide it for you."

He dropped down on his knee in front of her, slid a box from his pocket and opened it.

Inside was a diamond of elegant simplicity. He knew her. He knew she would never want the flashy ring, the large karat, the showpiece.

And he knew her answer.

He saw it in her eyes, in the tears that streamed down her face, in the smile that would not stop, despite the tears.

"Will you marry me?" he asked. "Will you make my world complete, Meredith?"

"Yes," she whispered. "Of course yes, a thousand times yes."

He rose to his feet, gathered her in his arms and held her. And his world finally was complete.

* * *

Meredith stared at herself in the mirror. She was in her slip at the dressing table, the bridal gown hung behind her. For a moment her eyes caught on it, and she felt a delicious quiver of disbelief.

Could this really be her life? A wedding gown out of a dream, yards and yards of ivory silk and seed pearls. Could this really be her life? Crowds had begun to form early this morning, lining the streets of Chatam from downtown all the way to Chatam Cathedral.

"You look so beautiful," Erin murmured.

Meredith gazed at the girl behind her.

Despite the pressure to have a huge wedding party, Meredith had chosen to have one attendant, Erin Fisher.

"So do you," she said.

"It's your day," Erin said, nonetheless pleased, "just focus on yourself for once, Miss Whit."

"All right."

"Now don't you look beautiful?"

She *did* look beautiful. More beautiful than she could have ever imagined she was going to look.

And it wasn't just the wedding gown, the hair, the makeup.

No, a radiance was pouring out of her, too big to contain within her skin.

"Are you crying?" Erin asked in horror. "Don't! We just did the makeup."

Meredith had been offered a room at the palace to get ready, and ladies in waiting to help her. She had said no to both. She wanted to be in this little apartment over her studio one last time. She wanted *her* girls to be around her.

Erin handed her a tissue and scolded. "I hope those are happy tears."

Meredith thought about it for a moment. "Not really, no."

"You are about to marry the most glorious man who ever walked and those aren't happy tears? Honestly, Miss Whit, I'm going to pinch you!"

"Don't pinch me. I might wake up."

"Tell me why they aren't happy tears."

"I was crying for the girl I used to be, the one who expected so little of life, who had such small dreams for herself. I was thinking of the girl who stood on those city hall steps, in a cheap dress, holding a tiny posy of flowers. I was thinking of the girl who felt so broken, as if it was her fault, some defect in her that caused him not to come, not to want to share the dream with her.

"If she could have seen the future she would have been dancing on those steps instead of crying. The truth? A different life awaited her. One that was beyond the smallness of her dreams."

"My dreams were so small, too," Erin whispered. "What would have become of me, if all that stuff hadn't happened to you? There would have been no Fairytale Ending group for me."

By vote, just last week, the girls, with Meredith's blessing, had changed the name of No Princes.

Because sometimes there just were princes.

And because, even when there weren't, everyone could make their own fairy-tale ending, no matter what.

"I think the universe has dreams for all of us that are bigger than what we would ever dare dream for ourselves," Meredith said quietly. "I even have to trust that losing my baby was part of a bigger plan that I will never totally understand. Maybe it made me stronger, deeper, more able to love. Worthy of that incredible man who loves me."

"Okay, stop!" Erin insisted, dabbing at her eyes. "My makeup is already done, too. Promise me, Miss Whit, that this day will be just about you and him. Not one more unhappy thought."

"All right," Meredith agreed, more to mollify the girl than anything else.

"We can't be walking down the cathedral aisle looking like a pair of raccoons," Erin said.

"Maybe you should have invested in waterproof makeup," a voice behind them said.

Erin whirled. "Prince Kiernan! Get out!" She tried to shield Meredith with her body. "You can't see her right now. It's bad luck."

"Luckily, I'm not superstitious. Could you give us a moment?"

For all the confidence she was developing, Erin wasn't about to make a stand with the prince of her country. She whirled and left the room.

Kiernan came up behind Meredith, rested his hand on her nearly naked shoulder. "This is pretty," he said touching her hair.

See? That was the problem with the promise she had made to Erin. This day could not be exclusively about the two of them.

"I thought it might be a little, er, too much," Meredith said, "but Denise is in hairdressing school. It was her gift to me. How can you refuse something like that?"

"You can't," he agreed. "Besides, it truly is beautiful."

"You really shouldn't be here," she chided him gently,

but the fact that he was here was so much better than a pinch.

This man was her life, her reason, her love, her reality.

"I had to see you," he said softly, "I have a gift for you and suddenly I realized that you needed to have it now, that I wanted you to have it close to your heart today."

All the gifts he had brought her over the course of their courtship could fill a small cottage. After they had become engaged, Meredith had quit asking him to stop. It filled him with such transparent joy to give her, a girl who had spent so much of her life with nothing, lovely things. She had learned to accept each gift graciously, because by doing so, she would receive the *real* gift.

His smile. A moment together in a busy, busy world. His touch on her arm. His eyes looking into her eyes with such wonder.

Now, Kiernan produced a small silver necklace, a cameo.

He pressed it into her hand, and she hesitated. When she touched a concealed button on the bottom of the locket it sprang open, revealing two tiny photos.

One was a picture of Carly, her head thrown back in laughter. And the other was a picture of her mother, looking young and strangely joyous.

"Where did you get this? My mother hated having her picture taken. And she so rarely looked like this, Kiernan. She looks so happy here."

"Ah, princedom has its privileges. I had the whole island scoured until I found just the right photos of both of them. Do you know when that was taken, Meredith? The picture of your mother?"

"No."

He named the date.

The tears spilled. The picture had been taken on the day of Meredith's birth.

"I wanted them to be with us," he said gently, "as close to your heart as I could get them."

"There goes the makeup," she accused him, and there went her idea that the day belonged to him and her, exclusively. What a selfish thought to entertain! This day belonged to Carly and her mother, too.

"You look better without it. The makeup."

"I know, but Rachel is in cosmetology."

"Let me guess. A gift?"

"Yes."

"And by accepting it, you *give* the gift just like the day you agreed to marry me."

The door to the room whispered open again.

"Kiernan! Out!"

There was no question of talking his way out of it this time, because it was his mother who had entered the room.

"Queen Aleda," Meredith said, truly surprised. "What are you doing here?" She had never been embarrassed about her tiny apartment, but she had certainly never expected to entertain a queen here, either.

"There are days when a girl needs her mother," the queen said. "Since your own cannot be here, I was hoping you would do me the grave honor of allowing me to take her place."

"Oh, Aleda," Meredith whispered. Of all the surprises of becoming Kiernan's love, wasn't his mother one of the best of them?

She was seen as reserved and cool, much as her son was. The truth about these two people? They guarded what was theirs, and chose very carefully who to give it to. And when they did give it?

It was with their entire hearts and whole souls.

Kiernan kissed her on her cheek, and bussed his mother, too, before quickly taking his leave. He left whistling *Get Me to the Church on Time*.

Queen Aleda quickly did what she did best—she took charge.

And Meredith realized, warmly, that this day belonged to Queen Aleda, too.

"None of that," Meredith was chastened for the new tears, "It will spoil your makeup."

Queen Aleda gathered the dress, hugged it to her briefly, looked at her soon-to-be daughter-in-law tenderly.

"Come," she said, "I'll help you get into it. The carriage will be here shortly."

Meredith was delivered to the cathedral in a white carriage, drawn by six white horses.

The people of Chatam, who seemed to have embraced her *more* for her past than less, lined the cobblestone streets, and threw rose petals in front of the carriage. The petals floated through the air and were stirred up by the horses' feet. It was as if it was snowing rose petals.

So, this day also belonged to them, to those people who had patiently lined the street for hours, waiting for this moment, a glimpse of the woman they considered to be *their* princess. They called her the people's favorite princess, and every day she tried to live up to what they needed from her. It had been a thought of pure selfishness to think this day was only about her and Kiernan.

The cathedral was packed. A choir sang.

And he waited.

At the end of that long, stone aisle, Kiernan waited

for her, strong, sure, ready. Her prince in a world she had once believed did not have princes, her very own fairy-tale ending.

Meredith moved toward him with the certainty, with the inevitability of a wave moving to shore.

And realized this day, and her whole life to follow, didn't really belong to her. And not to him, either.

It belonged to the force that had served them so well, the force that they would now use the days of their life serving.

It belonged to Love.

EPILOGUE

HE WENT HERE SOMETIMES, by himself, usually when he had a special occasion to celebrate. A birthday. An anniversary. They were part of it, and he could not leave them out.

It was not the nicest of graveyards, just row after row of simple crosses, no shrubs, or green spaces, no elaborate headstones, few flower arrangements.

The world would have been shocked, probably, to see Prince Kiernan of Chatam in this place, a grim, gray yard in the middle of Wentworth.

But he was always extra careful that he was not followed here, that no one hid with their cameras to capture this most private image of him.

It had become a most special place to him. He always brought flowers, two bouquets. He paused now in front of the heartbreakingly small grave, next to a larger one, brushed some dust from the plain stones set in the ground and read out loud.

"Carly, beloved." He set the tiny pink roses on her stone.

"Millicent Whitmore, beloved." He set the white roses there.

He did not know how the world worked. He felt a

tingle as he read that word. *Beloved.* How had a child long dead, whom he had never even met, become so beloved to him?

How could he feel as if he *knew* Millicent Whitmore, Millie as he called her affectionately, when he had never met her either?

Kiernan understood now, as he had not before marrying Meredith, that there was a larger picture, and despite his power and prestige he was just a tiny part of that.

He understood, as he had not before marrying Meredith, that sometimes great things could transpire out of great tragedies.

The death of a child, and her grandmother, had set a whole series of events in motion that not one single person could have ever foreseen or predicted.

Still, this is what love did: if he could give Meredith back her baby, even if it meant he would never meet her, and never have the life he had now, he would do it in a breath, in a heartbeat.

"I want you to know, Carly," he said softly, "that the new baby in no way replaces you. You are a sacred member of our family. Always and forever."

He felt her then, as he sometimes did, a breath on his cheek, a softness on his shoulder, a faint smell in the air that was so good.

"I brought you a picture of her. We've named her Amalee." He laid the picture, framed in silver, of his new baby and her mother between the two graves.

The picture he laid down was a private portrait, one that had never been released to the press. The baby had a wrinkled face, piercing gray eyes, and a tangle of the most shockingly red hair.

And Meredith in that picture looked like what she was: a mother who had already lost a child and would guard this one with a fierceness that was both awe-inspiring and a little frightening.

She looked like what she was: a woman certain in her own power, a woman who knew she was loved above all things.

Meredith was a woman who knew that if her husband ever had the choice to make: Chatam, his kingdom, or her, he would not even hesitate.

She was his kingdom.

He stepped back then, and sighed, asked silently for a blessing on the christening that would happen today, his baby's first public appearance. Already the people of Chatam lined the streets, waiting to welcome this new love to their lives.

He was left feeling humbled by the goodness of it all.

Each day his and Meredith's relationship became closer, deeper, stronger. The new baby, Amalee, felt as if she was part of a tapestry that wove his heart ever more intricately into its pattern.

Kiernan now knew, absolutely, what he had been so drawn to that first day that he had seen Meredith dance when she thought she was alone.

He had witnessed the dance of life.

And known, at a level that went so deep, that by-passed his mind and went straight to his heart, she was the one who could teach him the steps.

He learned a new one every day.

Love was a dance that you never knew completely,

that taught you new steps, that made you reach deeper and try harder.

Love was the dance that brought you right to heaven's door.

"Thank you," he whispered. And then louder. "Thank you."

MARCH 2011
HARDBACK TITLES

ROMANCE

A Stormy Spanish Summer	Penny Jordan
Taming the Last St Claire	Carole Mortimer
Not a Marrying Man	Miranda Lee
The Far Side of Paradise	Robyn Donald
Secrets of the Oasis	Abby Green
The Proud Wife	Kate Walker
The Heir From Nowhere	Trish Morey
One Desert Night	Maggie Cox
Her Not-So-Secret Diary	Anne Oliver
The Wedding Date	Ally Blake
The Baby Swap Miracle	Caroline Anderson
Honeymoon with the Rancher	Donna Alward
Expecting Royal Twins!	Melissa McClone
To Dance with a Prince	Cara Colter
Molly Cooper's Dream Date	Barbara Hannay
If the Red Slipper Fits...	Shirley Jump
The Man with the Locked Away Heart	Melanie Milburne
Socialite...or Nurse in a Million?	Molly Evans

HISTORICAL

More Than a Mistress	Ann Lethbridge
The Return of Lord Conistone	Lucy Ashford
Sir Ashley's Mettlesome Match	Mary Nichols
The Conqueror's Lady	Terri Brisbin

MEDICAL™

Summer Seaside Wedding	Abigail Gordon
Reunited: A Miracle Marriage	Judy Campbell
St Piran's: The Brooding Heart Surgeon	Alison Roberts
Playboy Doctor to Doting Dad	Sue MacKay

0211 Gen Std LP

MARCH 2011
LARGE PRINT TITLES

ROMANCE

The Dutiful Wife	Penny Jordan
His Christmas Virgin	Carole Mortimer
Public Marriage, Private Secrets	Helen Bianchin
Forbidden or For Bedding?	Julia James
Christmas with her Boss	Marion Lennox
Firefighter's Doorstep Baby	Barbara McMahon
Daddy by Christmas	Patricia Thayer
Christmas Magic on the Mountain	Melissa McClone

HISTORICAL

Reawakening Miss Calverley	Sylvia Andrew
The Unmasking of a Lady	Emily May
Captured by the Warrior	Meriel Fuller
The Accidental Princess	Michelle Willingham

MEDICAL™

Dating the Millionaire Doctor	Marion Lennox
Alessandro and the Cheery Nanny	Amy Andrews
Valentino's Pregnancy Bombshell	Amy Andrews
A Knight for Nurse Hart	Laura Iding
A Nurse to Tame the Playboy	Maggie Kingsley
Village Midwife, Blushing Bride	Gill Sanderson

MILLS BOON®

APRIL 2011
HARDBACK TITLES

ROMANCE

Jess's Promise	Lynne Graham
Not For Sale	Sandra Marton
After Their Vows	Michelle Reid
A Spanish Awakening	Kim Lawrence
In Want of a Wife?	Cathy Williams
The Highest Stakes of All	Sara Craven
Marriage Made on Paper	Maisey Yates
Picture of Innocence	Jacqueline Baird
The Man She Loves To Hate	Kelly Hunter
The End of Faking It	Natalie Anderson
In the Australian Billionaire's Arms	Margaret Way
Abby and the Bachelor Cop	Marion Lennox
Misty and the Single Dad	Marion Lennox
Daycare Mum to Wife	Jennie Adams
The Road Not Taken	Jackie Braun
Shipwrecked With Mr Wrong	Nikki Logan
The Honourable Maverick	Alison Roberts
The Unsung Hero	Alison Roberts

HISTORICAL

Secret Life of a Scandalous Debutante	Bronwyn Scott
One Illicit Night	Sophia James
The Governess and the Sheikh	Marguerite Kaye
Pirate's Daughter, Rebel Wife	June Francis

MEDICAL™

Taming Dr Tempest	Meredith Webber
The Doctor and the Debutante	Anne Fraser
St Piran's: The Fireman and Nurse Loveday	Kate Hardy
From Brooding Boss to Adoring Dad	Dianne Drake

APRIL 2011
LARGE PRINT TITLES

ROMANCE

Naive Bride, Defiant Wife	Lynne Graham
Nicolo: The Powerful Sicilian	Sandra Marton
Stranded, Seduced...Pregnant	Kim Lawrence
Shock: One-Night Heir	Melanie Milburne
Mistletoe and the Lost Stiletto	Liz Fielding
Angel of Smoky Hollow	Barbara McMahon
Christmas at Candlebark Farm	Michelle Douglas
Rescued by his Christmas Angel	Cara Colter

HISTORICAL

Innocent Courtesan to Adventurer's Bride	Louise Allen
Disgrace and Desire	Sarah Mallory
The Viking's Captive Princess	Michelle Styles
The Gamekeeper's Lady	Ann Lethbridge

MEDICAL™

Bachelor of the Baby Ward	Meredith Webber
Fairytale on the Children's Ward	Meredith Webber
Playboy Under the Mistletoe	Joanna Neil
Officer, Surgeon...Gentleman!	Janice Lynn
Midwife in the Family Way	Fiona McArthur
Their Marriage Miracle	Sue MacKay